INVASION TAIWAN

By

Eiji Oishi

Translated By

J.A. Buckley

Library and Archives Canada Cataloguing in Publication
Oishi, Eiji, author
Invasion Taiwan/Eiji Oishi

Issued in print and electronic formats.

ISBN: 978-1-998501-65-6 (paperback)
ISBN: 978-1-998501-66-3 (ebook)

Translated by: J. A. Buckley
Cover Design: Axel Peralta
Interior Design: Richa Bargotra

Double Dagger Books
Toronto, Ontario, Canada
www.doubledagger.ca

Naming Conventions

In this translation, Japanese names are presented in the Western order (given name followed by family name), while Chinese and Vietnamese names retain their customary order, with the family name appearing first.

'Senkaku Islands' is used as the default name for the Senkaku/Diaoyu Islands, given the story's Japanese origin. However, when referenced by Chinese or Taiwanese characters or from a Chinese perspective, the name 'Diaoyu Islands' is used. The largest island in the group is similarly referred to as 'Uotsuri Island' by default, switching to 'Diaoyu Island' when referenced from Chinese or Taiwanese perspectives.

'Pratas Island' is chosen over the Chinese name 'Dongsha Island' or the Japanese 'Tosa Island' as 'Pratas' is widely recognised as the international and neutral name.

Main Characters
(in order of appearance)

- ♀ Minami Komachi, university student and part-time convenience store employee living in Setagaya Ward, Tokyo
- Sachio Hamada, former Ground Self-Defense Force major, now Chief of the Kanto Area Business Continuity Plan
- Futoshi Tanaka, former Ground Self-Defense Force master sergeant, now a sales team member at the Hachioji Centre, western Tokyo
- Tetsuzo Akamine, President and CEO of the convenience store group
- Hiroshi Ito, former Ground Self-Defense Force colonel, graduate of Command and General Staff Course, stood up the Ground Self-Defense Force's cyber unit, former Director-General at the Ministry of Economy, Trade and Industry, doctorate in engineering, holds a government security clearance, nicknamed 'Echigo-ya'.
- Rear Admiral Shunji Kunishima, Commanding Officer, Escort Flotilla 1, Maritime Self-Defense Force
- Captain Tokuhiro Umehara, Chief of Staff, Escort Flotilla 1, Maritime Self-Defense Force
- Major General Kohei Domon, Commanding Officer, 403rd Headquarters Administrative Company (cover for the 'Silent Core' special forces unit), 1st Airborne Brigade,

and Temporary Commanding Officer, Amphibious Rapid Deployment Brigade, Ground Self-Defense Force

- Captain Takumi Harada, Platoon Commander, Amphibious Rapid Deployment Brigade, Ground Self-Defense Force
- Sergeant First Class Haruo Machida, callsign 'Garu', Harada Platoon, Amphibious Rapid Deployment Brigade
- Commander Song Qin, Commanding Officer, Jiaolong Assault Team, People's Liberation Army Navy Marine Corps
- Rear Admiral Ren Siyuan, Director, People's Liberation Army Special Operations Division, Operations Bureau, Joint Staff Department, and Commanding Officer, Special Warfare Command, People's Liberation Army Navy
- Senior Captain Ma Qinglin, Staff Officer, East Sea Fleet, People's Liberation Army Navy
- ♀ Commander Hao Fei, radar developer for the KJ-600 airborne early warning and control aircraft, People's Liberation Army Navy
- ♀ Lieutenant Commander Zhong Guilan, light detection and ranging system developer for the Y-9X patrol aircraft, People's Liberation Army Navy
- Dr. Zhang Gaoyuan, mathematician, S Agency
- Yusuke Shimoyama, former convenience store employee, former university football player
- Prime Minister Shiro Aso, Prime Minister of Japan
- Hiroshi Kuwabara, Parliamentary Vice-Minister of Defense, member of the National Defense Division, and member of the Japan-Taiwan Parliamentary Friendship Association
- General Yasuo Ushijima, Chief of Staff of the Ground Self-Defense Force
- Joe Stratton, Your Excellency, Counsellor for Government Affairs, Embassy of the United States, Tokyo

- Soichiro Katakura, Senior Deputy Minister for Foreign Affairs
- Koji Yasu, convenience store worker
- Commissioner Naoto Hiiragi, advisor to the National Cyber Unit, Kanto Regional Police Bureau
- ♀ First Lieutenant Kong Xueli, Vietnamese alias Nguyen Thi Lan, People's Liberation Army
- ♀ Dinh Lei Feng, Vietnamese collaborator
- Colonel Go Hakuba, Commanding Officer, 1st Amphibious Rapid Deployment Regiment, Amphibious Rapid Deployment Brigade, Ground Self-Defense Force
- ♀ Colonel Hikaru Shiba, Mandarin Chinese teacher and martial arts instructor for the Amphibious Rapid Deployment Brigade, Ground Self-Defense Force
- ♀ Lai Xiaochao, protégée of Colonel Hikaru Shiba
- Wang Wenxiong, also known as 'Fumio', graduate of Kyoto University's Faculty of Law, member of the Taiwan-Japan Goodwill Association, Deputy Director of the Kuomintang's Foreign Publicity Department
- Major General Sun Yougang, Operations Bureau, Joint Staff Department, People's Liberation Army
- Pan Hongda, Deputy Director, General Office of the Central Committee of the Chinese Communist Party
- ♀ Lieutenant Colonel Lin Hong, Japan Operations Unit, Joint Staff Department, People's Liberation Army
- ♀ Lieutenant Colonel Catherine Eiko Kitagawa, Intelligence Officer, Air Defense Command Headquarters, Air Self-Defense Force
- Colonel Minemitsu Habu, Team Leader, Operations Division Special Unit, Air Defense Command Headquarters, Air Self-Defense Force

- Commander Kunihiko Fukuhara, Systems Programs Division, Operations and Plans Department, Maritime Staff Office, Maritime Self-Defense Force
- Lieutenant Commander Kota Hinoue, P-1 pilot, Maritime Self-Defense Force
- Lieutenant General Takumi Maruyama, Commander, Air Defense Command, Air Self-Defense Force
- Major General Li Yan, Commanding Officer, 5th Tactical Fighter Wing, Republic of China (Taiwan) Air Force
- Lieutenant Colonel Liu Jianhong, Commanding Officer, 17th Flying Squadron, 5th Tactical Fighter Wing, Republic of China (Taiwan) Air Force
- Major General General Fu Xiangren, Commanding Officer, 601st Aviation Brigade, Republic of China (Taiwan) Army
- Major Ping Longyi, Commanding Officer, 1st Attack Squadron, 601st Aviation Brigade, Republic of China (Taiwan) Army
- ♀ Captain Lan Zhiling, AH-64E Apache Guardian attack helicopter pilot, 1st Attack Squadron, 601st Aviation Brigade, Republic of China (Taiwan) Army
- ♀ Second Lieutenant Tian Zuyi, AH-64E Apache Guardian attack helicopter gunner, 1st Attack Squadron, 601st Aviation Brigade, Republic of China (Taiwan) Army
- ♀ Lieutenant Colonel Keiko Togawa, Deputy Commander, Airborne Warning and Surveillance Group, Airborne Warning and Control Wing, Air Self-Defense Force
- Major Taiji Uchimura, Deputy Commander, 602nd Squadron, Airborne Warning and Surveillance Group, Air Self-Defense Force
- Terumi Saionji, Office for Disarmament Affairs, United Nations

- Li Fudong, Minister, Embassy of the People's Republic of China in Japan
- Sergeant Yan Cheng, Vietnamese alias Dang Quang Hao, People's Liberation Army
- Senior Captain Lei Yan, Operations Officer, 164th Marine Brigade, People's Liberation Army Navy, also known as the 'God of War'
- Commander Dai Yizhi, Intelligence Officer, 164th Marine Brigade, People's Liberation Army Navy
- Senior Captain Wan Yangdong, Chief of Staff, 164th Marine Brigade, People's Liberation Army Navy
- Rear Admiral Yao Yan, Commanding Officer, 164th Marine Brigade, People's Liberation Army Navy
- ♀ Major Elsie Chan, F-15EX pilot, United States Air Force, formerly of the Hawaii Air National Guard
- Lieutenant Colonel Masaaki Hidaka, Commanding Officer, 307th Provisional Squadron
- Lieutenant Colonel Oliver R. Evans, Operations Officer, 18th Wing, Kadena Air Base, and F-15EX instructor, United States Air Force
- ♀ Captain Ai Shinjo, F-15J/EX pilot, Air Self-Defense Force
- Vice Admiral Wang Zhihou (Retired), former Commanding Officer of the Republic of China (Taiwan) Marine Corps
- Ivan Tsurenko, Second Secretary, Embassy of the Russian Federation in Japan
- Gu Jinqiang, Defense Minister, Republic of China (Taiwan)
- Colonel Chen Zhiwei, Commanding Officer, 'Iron Force' 99th Brigade, Republic of China (Taiwan) Marine Corps
- Lieutenant Colonel Huang Junnan, Operations Officer, 'Iron Force' 99th Brigade, Republic of China (Taiwan) Marine Corps

- Major Wu Jinfeng, Intelligence Officer, 'Iron Force' 99th Brigade, Republic of China (Taiwan) Marine Corps
- Sergeant Liu Jinlong, callsign 'Dragon', 'Iron Force' 99th Brigade, Republic of China (Taiwan) Marine Corps

Prologue

A series of coincidences had left female university student Minami Komachi isolated amidst an unprecedented crisis. She had been drinking with friends in Shibuya until after eleven last night, and the trains were running as normal by the time she headed home.

At the restaurant, a group of salarymen at the table next to hers had been chatting about some war. She'd guessed it was probably the war between China and Taiwan. Two weeks ago, the Chinese People's Liberation Army had launched a surprise attack on Taiwan's Pratas Island south of the main island of Taiwan and now occupied it. Almost immediately after, rumours started circulating online saying that the PLA had landed on Japan's Uotsuri Island in the Senkaku Islands and were engaged in fierce fighting against the Self-Defense Forces. But that couldn't have been true, thought Minami. The Japanese government hadn't made any announcements, and there was nothing in the mainstream news about it either. They were probably just trolls trying to stir up drama.

Yesterday, the Japanese cabinet resigned en masse, but Minami didn't really understand the reason. She wasn't interested in politics, nor had she ever voted, and she doubted she ever would. When she woke up this morning, she noticed that the bathroom light was off and the fan wasn't working. She had no mobile phone or internet service either. She wondered if she was overdue on bills or something.

Minami also noticed that the normally noisy expressway near the Tomei Interchange was quiet. She could see that trucks were queued up bumper-to-bumper in what looked like a traffic jam; probably some kind of accident. Hungover and nursing her throbbing head, she quickly downed a cup of water to flush out the alcohol and lay back down. Her part-time shift didn't start until the evening. It would be an all-nighter, then tomorrow she had classes at university. But since the lecturer didn't take note of attendance, she would be more than fine to just sit at the back of the room and sleep.

Minami decided she would sleep until the afternoon. But just as she nodded off, she was woken up by the ringing of the doorbell by someone who had come up to her second level apartment. At first, she ignored it, figuring it was probably just a door-to-door salesman or something.

A child's voice called out, and Minami figured they might be some religious folks canvassing their belief. To drag a child into the missionary work of your own cult — how cruel, she thought. Naturally, she would ignore them.

But they didn't give up and were now knocking on the door, so Minami reluctantly got up. At the entryway she shouted, "I don't need anything!" and tried to go back to bed.

But on the other side a desperate voice called out, "Please, I'm not trying to sell you anything!"

She heard the child say, "Mama, can we go home?"

Now curious, Minami opened the door a crack with the chain still latched.

"Can I help you?"

"Hello, excuse me…I'm from the neighbourhood, and I was wondering if I could bother you for some hot water. It's for my baby's formula milk."

With her right hand, the woman thrust out a thermos flask, and with her left she was holding the hand of a boy who looked around three. The mother herself looked to be in her mid-thirties. She was dressed up as if she was going out, her makeup done nicely, and she was carrying the baby in a sling. The baby was little, perhaps only five months old, and sleeping peacefully, snuggled into mother's chest. This well-presented woman didn't look like someone who would struggle to pay her gas bill, and she didn't look like the kind of person who would live in this shabby apartment either. Minami unlatched the chain and opened the door. The little boy went to dash in.

"Stop there, darling! You can just go inside someone's house like that."

"You wanted hot water?"

"Yes, sorry. The electricity and gas are both out. But I wondered if you could still boil up water here since this apartment is on propane gas…I thought I could ask."

"There's a power outage?" Of course, that explained why the lights in her apartment wouldn't turn on. But why was the town gas cut off too? "Sure, I'll go boil some water. Just wait here."

Minami closed the door, filled a pot with water and lit the stove. She didn't have a proper kettle, just a single-handled pot for making ramen. The gas worked fine. She had never given it much thought, but this rundown apartment, precisely because it was rundown, still used traditional propane gas. She opened the door once again and stood at the entrance.

"Thank you so much and so sorry to bother you. There aren't too many people around here you can depend on."

"We live in a big, tall high-rise!" boasted the boy.

"A high-rise apartment? But they haven't built any high-rises in this area…"

"Oh, it's one of those high-rises along the Tama River. My husband has this hobby, you know, using a telescope to watch common people below go about their lives — I mean, no offence! So he remembered this old, somewhat rundown apartment in the area that still uses propane gas cylinders."

"Umm, right…?"

There was nothing really to object to. It was technically the truth.

"Oh, I don't mean he's been spying into your apartment or anything. Your apartment is north facing, and our high-rise is on the opposite side. But even though we live in a high-rise, our apartment faces north too. The ones with a view of the fireworks over the Tama River had long odds in the lottery, and we didn't win. Not that we couldn't afford it," the mother explained, looking somewhat regretful.

"So there's a power outage? When did that happen?"

"You don't know?"

"No. I was out late last night."

"You didn't see the prime minister's address or anything?"

"What time was that?"

"Yesterday evening. He declared we're in a state of war with China. The SDF has been mobilised. And there's a rumour going around that the Soviet army has come back again and they've landed at Niigata! An army of tanks will be coming through the Usui Pass before long!"

"The Soviet army? As in the Soviet Union?"

"Yes, but it was my neighbour who told me that. She's the wife of the former head of a government office, and she's a bit cray-cray, so maybe don't take it as fact."

"But it's true then shouldn't we be fleeing? Rather than staying here like this?"

"We considered that, but at any rate, the Tomei Expressway, Kanpachi-dori Avenue, National Route 246, all of them are completely gridlocked. Terrible traffic jams. Even with my husband driving our Audi, taking all sorts of backstreets, we barely made it to this cluttered downtown area. Do you not watch the news?"

"I don't have a TV or a radio. Just my phone."

"Young people these days, I guess…Our building does have a backup generator, but it's mainly for operating the elevators and the pumps for water and sewage. We don't have any power inside our apartment. That's the thing about high-rises, isn't it? We can't use gas appliances; we only have induction cookers."

———

In the distance a fire truck siren was sounding. They were announcing something on a megaphone, but Minami couldn't make out the words.

"Is there any help from the government or something?"

"Yes. But where's the community centre around here? I wouldn't know where to find one. Or even where the local primary school is. All the children in my neighbourhood go to private schools. If I were to ask my neighbours where the public schools were, none of them would know."

Primary schools usually served as polling stations for elections, so any typical adult would know where they were, Minami thought to herself. But then again, she never bothered to vote herself. She wouldn't have minded listening to a bit more boasting from the upper class, but since the water had boiled, she took the thermos and filled it.

"Thank you so much! Here, please take this as a token of gratitude." The mother then held out a neatly folded ten-thousand yen note.

"Oh, please no. It's just hot water."

"No, please take it. But I do ask…We don't know how long the power will be out, so I may have to call on you for help again."

Indeed, Minami thought, this kind of brazenness must be the secret to climbing the social ladder. Just then, she suddenly remembered something.

"So you can't use gas appliances at all at your high-rise?"

"We just can't get them installed as kitchen appliances. They don't mind us using portable gas stoves. I raced to the convenience store first thing this morning to get one, but they were completely sold out. And in any case, our kids are too small for hotpots or barbequed meat. Sometimes the residents put on glamping parties in the courtyard. They pitch tents and decorate them with lights for nighttime and have barbecues."

Minami popped back inside her apartment and fetched a portable stove and two gas canisters from the kitchen storage shelf. "I haven't used these lately. One of the canisters should be completely full and unused. They should last a few days if you just use it to boil water for baby formula."

The mother was taken aback. "You're giving me this? Are you sure?"

"We'll be able to use the propane gas here for a while, so I don't need it right now. Please take it. For the baby." Minami then put them into an old tote bag.

Tears welled up in the mother's eyes. In a flurry, she took out a Louis Vuitton purse from her back pocket. "Please accept this."

Minami's eye's bulged in astonishment at the sight of around twenty ten-thousand yen notes in the mother's purse. The mother then tried to give her ten of them.

"Not a chance. How about I just take the ten-thousand yen note from before?"

"No, that won't sit well with me. My husband will be upset too. Besides, you never know what might happen next, so isn't it better to have more cash on hand? Think of it as a twist of fate. Please accept it."

"Well, I'll accept half of it then, fifty-thousand yen," Minami said and accepted the cash.

"We're the Nirasawas, from Tower B over there. If you ever need anything, please do come by. The building association should at least have a stockpile of biscuits. It's a bit of a walk from here, though. And we shall invite you to the summer fireworks festival. The party room on the top floor will be open."

"Thank you so much. Please take care."

"Bye-bye," said the little boy as he waved his hand.

I guess even annoying rich people's kids are cute too, thought Minami. As the mother descended the stairs she kept turning around to bow.

"Be careful going down the steps!" Minami called.

A car pulled up. Her husband who was driving a classy, foreign car gave a quick nod from the driver's seat. Perhaps they figured that a mother and child would be more likely to have doors opened for them than a man.

All Minami could think was that, although they belonged to a social class she would never be part of, the child was completely innocent. And she wondered what would have happened had she demanded all the cash in the mother's purse. And the distance from that high-rise by the river to here, even as the crow flies, must be over two kilometres. What kind of person satisfied their curiosity by observing the lives of ordinary people below through a telescope from a high-rise? And war with China? What kind of nonsense was that?

Japan was, in fact, in a state of war with China. The PLA had conducted a lightning occupation of Taiwan's Pratas Island,

and in response, Japan Maritime Self-Defense Force submarines supported a covert operation to evacuate Taiwanese forces from the island. Though not explicitly as retaliation, Chinese forces had landed on Japan's Uotsuri Island in the Senkaku Islands, which China referred to as Diaoyu Island in the Diaoyu Islands, as part of the second phase of their Taiwan invasion strategy.

The MSDF had expended several Aegis ships' worth of missiles, and, the Japan Air Self-Defense Force fighters had sortied hundreds of times to engage in the air. Many Chinese warships had been sunk.

The SDF threw its military might into battle after battle with a small number of Taiwanese forces also getting involved. Despite suffering heavy casualties, the Japan Ground Self-Defense Force's Amphibious Rapid Deployment Brigade finally managed to drive out the landed PLA forces and successfully retake Uotsuri Island.

However, this battle, merely a phase in the conflict over the Senkaku Islands, was just the conclusion of the first stage. China was already gearing up for its next confrontation with Taiwan and Japan.

In a campaign of unrestricted warfare against Japan, China had destroyed electrical power sources, had operatives infiltrate transformer substations sites and blow them up, blown up undersea cable landing stations, and shattered the power supply network to the Tokyo Sky Tree, knocking out both television and radio services. Even satellite television was off the air, leading to a complete blackout across the entire Japanese archipelago.

Taiwan was in a similar state.

In Tokyo last night, the moment the train services stopped with the last trains, the entire Kanto region experienced a power outage. Before dawn, the internet was completely down.

Mobile phone services were disrupted, and as a result, landline services were overwhelmed and completely paralysed during the daytime period. Serpentine queues had formed at the few functioning public payphones.

And female university student, Minami Komachi, had been completely unaware of any of this for the first half of the day.

1

The Convenience Store

Sachio Hamada, former GSDF major and now Chief of the Kanto Area Business Continuity Plan, stood by a screen at the front of the Tokyo Store Centre reception hall inside a Shinjuku skyscraper. He was chatting to people who had gathered for the first re-union in a long time.

The room was without electric light, illuminated only by the natural light from outside. The air was stagnant, thick with humidity, and oppressively sultry. The people here carried themselves differently from regular business folk. Their ages varied, and at first glance, they could be mistaken for a group of salespeople, but all of them had short haircuts and were well-tanned. They stood, backs straight, and conversed pleasantly, but there was no idle chatter. When one started to speak, the others would stop and listen in carefully. Close to a hundred men and maybe ten women were there.

"Tanaka, how did you get here from the Hachioji Centre? That's forty k's away. Were you already in the area or something?"

"No, I came here with a friend using one of those rent-a-cycles. I took regular roads." Futoshi Tanaka, a former GSDF master sergeant who was a sales team member at the Hachioji Centre in the western outskirts of Tokyo, was nonchalant in his response. "I could have biked down the Chuo Expressway, but it's not for everyone. The journey here took less than two hours. Expecting three for the way back, though, with bags and traffic and all. And no battery power on the bike."

"Be careful on those things. We're not getting any younger."

"Sure. I jog ten k's to work everyday. No issues with stamina here. I've got a pump and puncture repair kit with me too."

"I wish I could do the same, but the air quality is terrible around here, not to mention the traffic."

When two men in business suits appeared at the door, everyone stood to attention then bowed respectfully.

"Let's not make this too formal. Please have a seat everyone," said Tetsuzo Akamine, President and CEO of the group, standing next to Hamada.

"Well, I somehow made it from Ozaki HQ in one piece. Clung for dear life to the back of a young speedster on a motorbike. Every road was jammed up. You all seem to have got here fine, no signs of distress? I expected no less from you pros.

"Anyway, where do I begin? Our convenience store group. I heard we first started hiring retired SDF officials around about the time the bubble economy collapsed in the early nineties. Convenience stores were opening up everywhere back then. There were quite a few naysayers from what I heard. 'Sure these military folk understood etiquette, kept strictly to timings and could push through anything. But should we hire people in their late thirties or forties, a generation set in their ways? Would they really be useful?' That was the criticism I heard. But you all proved to be a valuable force, especially during the 3-11 disaster. You've all got a knack for crisis response, which not only saved our company, but also made significant contributions to society.

"You know, the convenience store is now an indispensable part of the national infrastructure. During this unprecedented crisis we're now in, we have a higher calling, and the ability to make a difference. This is our duty. I call upon each of you to lead the way." Akamine turned to Hamada and asked, "By the way, does this gathering have a name?"

"It's called 'The Sakura Society'. It was formed in 2011, six months after 3-11 by a veterans employment organisation as a study group to learn from experiences during the triple disaster."

"Store managers I've spoken to today can't believe you Sakura Society people managed to set up direct fax lines to the company with the regular phone and internet services down and all. We've got a lot to thank you for already. If it weren't for your initiative and ability to take action, our convenience stores would be in the dark right now. Now we just have to be patient until the road conditions improve and the networks are restored. Delivery vans are already on the move, but the situation is much like 3-11. So please keep giving your all. We're depending on you.

"You'll be going from one isolated convenience store to another in towns with no information and no electricity, turning on the lights, providing clear direction, delivering essential supplies, and saving lives. This is a big deal for the nation and the people. And for the company, and for us as professionals. It's a monumental task, the likes of which we hope not to experience again…Anyway, I hope that is motivation enough for you? Over to you, Mr. Hamada."

"Much obliged, Mr. Akamine. Now, everyone, please open the operation folders on the tables. The operation is called the 'Kanda River Clean-up Plan'. Let me start by saying that we anticipate a worsening of the security situation, which means you have to strictly abide by the two-person rule during the day. After dark, operate in groups of four if possible, or at least in groups of three. Do not carry any weapons — no metal bats or anything. If you encounter danger, focus on escaping whatever way you can. Survival is your number one priority.

"We've invited a guest from the government as well, so please ensure to extend a proper greeting. Some of you might have worked with him before, but unlike us regulars, he's a former colonel and graduated from the Command and General Staff Course. He also has a doctorate in engineering. Our cyber security branch tried to scout him, but the salary wasn't enough, I hear." Hamada passed the floor to a man wearing glasses.

"Actually, it wasn't a matter of salary," said former GSDF colonel Hiroshi Ito, softly refuting the claim.

"Ladies and gents. I learnt all my skills during my time as an SDF officer. All taxpayer funded, including my training and research. After I separated from the forces for personal reasons, I ventured into the private sector for a brief period. I did hesitate quite a bit before I made that jump, though. A good part of me felt the knowledge I'd acquired should inherently be returned to society for the public good, rather than help line the pockets of private business.

"Anyway, I first learnt of the Sakura Society during my time as Director-General at the Ministry of Economy, Trade and Industry. Mr. Hamada approached me asking if there was any support the government could provide. Since then, we've worked out the finer details, established cross-industry networking groups, and used these to set up systems to allow collaboration between rival companies. The delivery teams currently doing the rounds are also carrying products from rival stores.

"Each of you has amassed knowledge and experience in the less glamorous fields like logistics and finance in the land, sea, and air domains. And you've developed the very military characteristic of adaptability. I received a message from the prime minister, too, expressing his hopes for your activities.

The situation is extremely severe. The Tokyo Metropolitan Government has formed a bicycle corps to maintain comms with the ward offices, since patrol cars and fire engines are unable to move quickly enough.

"The 'so what' of all this is that the government has prepared for this hybrid war, and utilising convenience stores is one part of the plan. Post offices are not always located in convenient places, the same goes for ward offices, elementary schools, and community centres. But in urban areas, convenience stores are everywhere. If you walk around any neighbourhood for any amount of time, you're almost guaranteed to come across a convenience store. The strategy now is to use these convenience stores as a lifeline for information.

"We don't know how long this will last; there's no timeline or estimate in terms of days. We have no idea how long it will take to restore electricity, radio and TV broadcasting, or internet services. For now, do your best to serve as the local information hub for at least the next three days.

"In regards to the labour shortage, we're preparing ways to recruit a volunteer workforce. The ops plan doesn't cover everything, and, naturally, we anticipate there'll be things not written on paper. Whether or not this goes smoothly hinges largely on your actions.

"We've prepared items here for you to take back. Inside these fifty-litre backpacks, there are over ten kilos of supplies — a disassembled megaphone, nutritional jelly for children, portable toilets, women's sanitary products, and more. In the front basket of the rent-a-cycle, we'll have you put five litres, or five kilos' worth, of formula. You can use the rent-a-cycle battery if you want, that's fine. For today, every convenience store will be equipped with UPS power supply units, and some will get fuel-cell generators. You can recharge with those. There are also chargers in this building. It's quite heavy, take care riding and try not to get a flat. The Tokyo police are saying that because of fuel shortage, the traffic situation should ease by tomorrow, although this could be one of those wild rumours going around. The latest fake news story we've heard is that a unit of tanks from the old Soviet Army will soon make its way through the Usui Pass.

"Alright, I'll leave the rest to you, Mr. Hamada. If anything comes up, use the usual channel." Ito finished talking and moved over by the company president. As they departed, the room stood and bowed in a very military, or rather, a very SDF manner.

Akamine and Ito descended the staircase and headed towards one of the company's convenience stores. A convenience store in name only, it was actually a training and development facility, so there were no customers. The products on display were identical to those in a regular store, complete with a cash register, kitchen, copier, and ATM. The ATM wasn't connected to any network and just operated a simulation.

An employee was inside by the open automatic door, attempting to affix a notice made of a row of four A4 sheets. In large font it read, HOW TO MAKE A SIMPLE OIL LANTERN USING SALAD OIL.

"Well, I guess all the candles sold out last night," commented Ito.

"Not just candles. When I visited some stores earlier, even the extra spicy ramen was sold out — and that stuff never sells! I wonder how people are making hot water with the gas cut off? But what really surprises me is that, even though it's cash only at the moment, we're still selling everything out. I guess Japanese people really do love their cash…"

"Well, we are a country that faces massive disasters every few years." Ito then turned to the employee putting up the notice, "Oh, sorry, please don't put it up on the inside of the window.

Follow the manual and stick it up on the outside. If you put it up like that it'll be hard to see with the reflection of the outside light, and you won't be able to see it at all at night. Also, raise it another fifty centimetres. Elderly people can't read notices low down without stooping."

"Ito, next thing you know you'll be a store manager!"

Upon entering the pseudo store, they saw a middle-aged man in work clothes at the cash register counter, tilting his head as he worked with his hands. On a table, various products from the store had been opened and laid out, from empty cup noodle containers to duct tape and earphones.

"This is our chief engineer. He worked for an audio equipment manufacturer for forty years. We finally managed to track him down last week and got him to hear us out," explained Ito to the company president.

"Is this some kind of handicraft?"

"A megaphone. We're giving them proper megaphones, but we're also challenging him to create instructions for a DIY megaphone using store products that can be written on a single piece of paper."

Next to the engineer, a young employee drenched in sweat was busy assembling something. He had wrapped a ballpoint pen in nichrome wire which appeared to have been stripped from some cord.

"Remember the movie *Apollo 13*? The astronauts took refuge in the lunar module, but the carbon dioxide levels kept rising. They managed to create a makeshift air purifier using parts they had in the module. This is the same kind of thing here. Isn't that right, Uga?"

"Yessir. It's quite easy to make a megaphone speaker yourself. There are DIY videos about it on YouTube. Connect this to the headphone jack of a smartphone and you have yourself a speaker.

You'll need a magnet, but you can get those from the door of a hot drink or coffee maker. The main problem is the power output. It chews up a lot of battery. You can find everything from scissors to cutters in the store. We don't sell solders or soldering irons, but you can still put one together without those."

"Keep up the good work." Akamine turned back to Ito, "So you can pretty much make anything yourself?"

"That's right. You can make things like flashlights, lighters, transceivers, or defibs using only products in the store. Back in the transistor era you could do more of the impossible; integrated circuits these days make it harder."

"Can't you just roll up a piece of cardboard to make a megaphone?" asked Akamine.

"I'm sure they'll resort to those as well. You know, the Ministry of Culture and local authorities are working to recruit local high school students to form information units?"

"Will that work?"

"Well, believe it or not, the primary mission objective is not exactly to deliver accurate information to residents. During times like these, rumours tend to spread. Subversive operatives that have infiltrated the country will try to spread rumours and such. So what can we do? It's difficult to ensure only the correct information is disseminated. So, the alternative is to immerse the public in a sea of information. Keep providing them with information, leaving no time for them to think. It's a propaganda technique used by totalitarian states, actually. The Nazis employed it long ago."

At the end of the counter, a simple lantern made with salad oil floating in a paper cup was burning. It was made by twisting tissue paper into a very thin strand, wrapping it in aluminium foil, and then standing it on the oil.

"What's this 'Tokyo Tower 20:00'?"

"Best keep that one a secret for now. It's a surprise for later," said Ito with a suggestive grin. They had printed a heap of notices from the copier with the intent to post them later. At the bottom of each notice, TOKYO TOWER 20:00 had been printed in red.

Uga connected a smartphone to the finished megaphone and tested the sound. While it did produce sound, it was rather distorted, and the volume was, at best, no different from the smartphone's own maximum volume. "We may have to call on locals to provide soldering irons. Still plenty of room for improvement."

"Mr. Uga, once this upheaval has settled, let's start a business making emergency evacuation kits out of convenience store products. Wish I'd thought about it sooner!" The company president thanked Uga with a bow before leaving the store. Outside, tables and a whiteboard had been set up for those attending the tutorials after the training session.

"Ito, may I have a moment to discuss something? To be honest, I'm quite lost…Being thrown into such a total information desert, we might end up believing anything, even rumours like the Red Army crossing Usui Pass. Is the government really handling things well? Has the Chinese military already begun its landing on Taiwan?"

"No, that hasn't happened yet, but it's only a matter of time. Honestly, I never expected they could cyber attack satellite TV. They're being thorough and merciless. And to think the Skytree was cut off not just from the power grid but also from the broadcast networks."

"Roughly speaking, how long will it take to recover? We can pride ourselves on being part of the public infrastructure all we want, but there are limits. The shelves are already empty."

"Three days, including today. They estimate at least three days until the power grid is recovered. TV and radio services might be back up a bit quicker if they push for it hard enough. But no one will have access unless the power comes back. The government has a program called an ESF — Emergency Support Function. I helped with its formation. It's by no means perfect, but it should function more effectively than during the 3-11 triple disaster."

"I have a favour to ask…" Akamine took two crumpled A4 pieces of paper from his suit pocket, opened them up and showed Ito. Handwritten words densely filled the paper in the form of product lists. "We scrambled to put this together at headquarters, but I have no idea how or to whom to submit it. It's a list of products needed at the stores. We're still in comms with the suppliers, but they can't get the products out."

"I'll take care of it. But no need for concern. The Business Continuity Plan chief has already considered and itemised things like the ones written here. We've worked out where the logistical bottlenecks are. But please trust them. If the supply chains that allow continuous support to convenience stores are combined with the SDF's experience in combat logistics, we'll get a good result."

"You think so? I hadn't heard about it at all. I didn't think a BCP would be at all necessary during my tenure as president, unless there was a major earthquake in Kanto or something."

"Well, you'll have your name written in the annals of convenience stores…an industry leader who supported the country during conflict. You might even get a medal for your efforts!"

"Well, let's hope Japan survives…" muttered Akamine with a grave expression on his face, an expression that revealed a feeling of despair for the developing situation.

———

The 10,250-tonne Japan Ship *Maya* Aegis destroyer of MSDF Escort Flotilla 1 came alongside the so-called Naha Military Port on the main island of Okinawa and took on supplies from the mobile supply unit.

It was the first time since before the conflict the ship had returned to this port without having fired off a missile. During one of the engagements, she had exhausted her missile arsenal within minutes and was forced into the dire situation of having to use her main gun to shoot down incoming enemy missiles. It was a miracle that the escort fleet was unharmed. They had completed their mission to defend the Senkaku Islands, intercepting every single missile that was launched.

After their missile stores were depleted, the ships would race back here, reload with missiles airlifted from the U.S., then head back to patrol near the Senkaku Islands in a continuous cycle.

The GSDF was successful in retaking Uotsuri Island, the PLA completing their withdrawal the morning of the previous day. However, the PLA had managed to capture an MSDF air-cushioned landing craft and a small number of Chinese troops were heading back to the Chinese mainland with it. And on board this landing craft were some very special prisoners of war — a group of senior Japanese officers from the GSDF's Amphibious Rapid Deployment Brigade who had been captured in an ambush just before landing. The brigade's commander, also one of the POWs, was forced to read a humiliating statement on camera which China then broadcast to the world.

The Japanese government only publicly disclosed the situation on Uotsuri Island with the resignation of the entire cabinet and the inauguration of the new administration, and at the same time, issued a retrospective defence mobilisation order. The opposition party criticised the fact that the SDF had deployed and operated without a formal mobilisation order, but with the nation forced into a blackout, it was difficult to gauge the public's opinion on the matter.

Naturally, in China, information about the failed mission to land on and occupy the Senkaku Islands was not made public at all. But the population's morale was boosted by scenes of the captured Japanese major general humiliatingly announcing 'defeat'.

Escort Flotilla 1 Commanding Officer Rear Admiral Shunji Kunishima and his Chief of Staff, Captain Tokuhiro Umehara, stood on the starboard wing of the *Maya*, watching the GSDF vehicle drive away from the seawall. In the adjacent area, the GSDF's Patriot missile units deployed at Camp Naha were set up to protect the harbour, their launchers facing the East China Sea.

"Had you heard of Major General Domon before, sir?"

"That was the first I'd heard of him, not that I've ever paid much attention to the list of GSDF generals. They say that sometimes GSDF officers who haven't officially left the SDF suddenly disappear from the list. Usually something to do with Special Forces Group."

This visitor from the GSDF had come on board to thank them for their efforts in the defence of Uotsuri Island. Rear Admiral Kunishima had originally assumed that the operation was commanded by the commander of the Amphibious Rapid Deployment Brigade, but this visit from the Special Force Group two-star seemed to indicate otherwise.

The GSDF forces had faced repeated saturation attacks from ground-attack missiles aimed at the western end of Uotsuri Island, where they had taken up positions. The *Maya* and her sister ship JS *Haguro* intercepted and shot down these missiles.

They had executed their mission flawlessly; not one of the enemy's missiles was allowed to hit its target. With each barrage they expended all their missile stores, launching missiles in sea states much heavier than they were used to.

As the ships swayed violently, fire from the pitching missiles scorched the hulls. Areas around the hulls were now charred, paint burnt off, and rust was already beginning to appear. The intensity of the battle was also evident in the damage to the bridge structure.

The Naha Military Port was off-limits, but the damage to the *Maya* was clearly visible from a park across the port. Although with the internet down, the extent of the damage remained unknown to the wider public.

Across Japan the power was out and the mobile phone network was down, but Okinawa was the exception. The power did go out across the island for a moment at the beginning, but after only an hour it was restored. Although the Okinawa Electric Power Company did not officially acknowledge it, the core system there suffered a cyber-attack and was temporarily knocked out, but after an hour it seemed to come back online by itself.

The MSDF's cyber unit assessed that whoever initiated the cyber-attack likely had free control over the power supply system. This meant that, even now, the core system remained in the enemy's hands and that Beijing could cut off the power to Okinawa at its time of choosing. The key question was why was it not doing so now?

Okinawa was the sole region in Japan where television and radio could broadcast unobstructed. The media was reporting on the situation on mainland Japan continuously, even though there was no connection to the mainland available. But the fact that television was broadcasting was significant. Okinawa's media had historically been critical of the central government, the SDF and the U.S. military. It was thought that allowing continuous broadcast of the nationwide blackout aimed to instil in the Okinawan population a sense of futility and wastefulness in striking back at China, and that keeping Okinawa online was a deliberate move for this purpose. In fact, at that moment a citizen's group ensconced at the front gate of the Naha Military Port and demanding an end to the war was eyeing off against riot police.

"What do you think will happen if we involve ourselves in the defence of Taiwan?" asked Umehara.

"I don't even want to think about it. If that happens, China won't hesitate to launch ballistic missiles against Kadena Air Base and this port. It won't be a friendly volley of missiles like last time; it'll be a saturation attack. With two Aegis ships, we could probably only manage twenty intercepts here. Maybe even fewer. The bases will be paralysed for at least half a day. If Kadena's attacked, the U.S. Air Force will have to take the long road and sortie from Andersen Air Base on Guam. But if they attack Kadena, it's safe to say they'll target Andersen too. Then the U.S. will lose its key air bases for the defence of Taiwan. If that happens, it's just us and the U.S. 7th Fleet — if they decide to turn up — and we might not be able to hold out for long. We managed to defend the Senkakus, but the defence of Taiwan feels like a losing battle from the start."

"Well, we've rested for a day. Let's hope tomorrow is peaceful too."

"I know we can't grant the crew leave, but hopefully with each ship taking turns to dock for resupply and replenishment they can get some physical and mental down time after that ordeal. It's crucial."

A destroyer appeared outside the port, waiting to enter. It was time for the *Maya* to clear the space and set out.

———

Major General Kohei Domon, who commanded the GSDF 1st Airborne Brigade's 403rd Headquarters Administrative Company, cover for the *Silent Core* special forces unit, retreated to a small conference room in the Camp Naha Headquarters Administration building.

With the Amphibious Brigade's commander captured, Domon had taken temporary command of the unit that had deployed to Uotsuri Island.

Last night, for the first time in quite a while, the entire unit was able to bathe. They managed to take off their dirty gear and wash their combat uniforms and other items. Instead of sleeping on the ground, they were allowed to sleep on beds, albeit hard ones. Once dawn broke, they spent their time tending to their equipment. They replaced the barrels of their assault and sniper rifles, swapped out the batteries in radios and LED signal lamps, and fixed up their FAST combat helmets by replacing the inner padding and repairing the outer velcro and rail systems, all in preparation for the next engagement.

The garrison was virtually empty, with only a few security platoons and the Patriot missile unit remaining. The infantry had already evacuated the base in full gear in anticipation of missile attacks. Not even Major General Domon knew where they had concealed themselves.

Captain Takumi Harada, one of the platoon commanders, returned from an outing. He was dressed not in combat uniform or service dress, but in casual sweatshirt and trousers so as not to alarm the local residents.

"Where did you go again?" asked Domon.

"City hospital, sir. To check in on the injured. There were some with serious injuries who couldn't be moved, but I briefly updated those who were conscious on the overall situation."

Captain Harada was a commando with a medic background, and had nursing qualifications and specialised skills in satellite communications.

"Any issues?"

"No, sir. The experience with COVID has significantly improved our life-saving techniques, and this has also benefited trauma care. But because of this blackout, I can't get updates on the severely injured guys — the ones with burns and the like — who were sent back to the mainland, some to that university hospital in Kansai…"

"Places like that should have their own power supply, so they'll be alright for the time being. I hear Ito is at the PM's Office taking care of things, so I'm not too worried."

"It's unusually quiet here. Will the troops not be returning?"

"Missiles can come flying in from mainland China in minutes. Given the size of the garrison, it's simply not possible to evacuate this place in a matter of minutes."

"Are we okay with that? The Japanese military will be criticised again for abandoning civilians."

"The local units can figure out how to explain it. If a unit is wiped out, there won't be any helping those that need help anyway. Keep your bags packed at all times; we have to be able to evacuate in two minutes." Domon turned to Sergeant First Class Haruo Machida, known as *Garu*, who was arranging computers and monitors by the window. "Garu, can we carry this system out in two minutes?"

"Yessir, I can certainly show you. Fold the computer monitor, detach the radio antenna, unplug it from the wall socket, sling the cables round my neck, throw it all into this massive coin laundry basket and carry it all out. I reckon thirty seconds to have my own gear on my shoulders, and sixty seconds to toss this whole system into the basket."

"Understood. Hmm, so for unit sustainment, I've got Kan's platoon resting up the road at Camp Kinser. They've borrowed some space from the U.S. Marines there."

"Do you have any updates, sir?" asked Harada.

"We're in comms with the mainland forces, no real issues there. The SDF's dedicated lines do drop out occasionally, but the satellite connections are still operational, and for us, satellite-based internet has also become available. Garu, show him something, will you?"

Garu displayed the CNN website on his computer. "Japanese sites are down, of course, but sites from the U.S. mainland can be accessed without any problems."

Harada was surprised, "That loaded fast! Is this the same internet connection as on passenger planes?"

"Well, not all satellite services are the same. The internet on passenger planes mostly uses geostationary satellites with narrow bandwidths, they even struggle sending and receiving text data. Even email can be annoyingly slow. The Kirameki satellites used exclusively by the SDF operate in geo orbit too, but we're not allowed to use those for internet. The satellite I'm connected to now is part of a low Earth orbit service from a satellite constellation project aimed at providing cheap internet to remote areas that don't have fixed lines or mobile networks. It's pretty quick, comparable to broadband speeds. But China will probably end up interfering with it too. It's not particularly resistant to hacking, so I don't expect to be able to use it for long."

"So, if we take this to Uotsuri Island, could we use the internet like normal there?"

"Absolutely, no problem. It's not as cheap or fast as a mobile phone plan, but nothing a platoon commander's monthly wage couldn't afford," Machida said with a cheeky grin. Machida showed Harada the device connected to the computer. It was about the size of a smartphone, smaller than the mobile satellite phones that they usually carried around. It didn't even have a peripheral satcom antenna connected to it.

"Nowadays, even newer iPhones can connect to low Earth orbit satellites."

"Amazing…" Harada turned to Domon and asked, "So, are we going to Taiwan, sir?"

"I'm not sure. This prime minister doesn't have any particular affinity to Taiwan, nor does he hold negative views. The Japan-Taiwan parliamentary group will huff and puff, and I doubt China will back down next time. If Japan gets involved, it might be after Taiwan has lost control of the air and the PLA has landed. If we intervene under those circumstances, it won't just be about the Amphibious Brigade anymore. It would mean a real war staged in Taiwan. This would clearly be unconstitutional, and I can't see it as something we can respond to under the current law which is all about so-called perilous situations around Japan. The Joint Staff Office has started making maps of Taiwan, which we're downloading daily to be ready for any landing orders. That's why we're still in Okinawa.

"But before any of that, there's the matter of evacuating Japanese nationals. Twenty-thousand Japanese live in Taiwan. Most of them have already left, but thousands remain. The Ministry of Foreign Affairs' representative office there is apparently working on a plan to advise people where they should gather if push comes to shove, as in, where the buses will be to get them out of Taipei. But given the risks in controlling the air, I don't see how they'll be able to meet the helicopters on the east coast and fly out. The challenge is not just about us getting there and buying time; it's also the sheer numbers, including Taiwanese, that will rush in." Domon turned to Machida. "Make sure you order the necessary medical and sanitary supplies. Was there anything else?"

"Well, there was the matter of Mrs Harada, sir."

"Oh, that's right, your wife, Harada! I had Sergeant First Class Amari back in Narashino go and pick her up and take her to the barracks."

Harada, looking puzzled, "To our barracks back at Camp Narashino? My wife is a civilian."

"And she's Chinese!"

"That makes it even more…odd?"

"But she has Japanese citizenship, doesn't she? Didn't I arrange for her citizenship and registration in the family register? I can't really remember. Anyway, our barracks back there near Tokyo is officially just a warehouse and parachute equipment building. Right now she's in my office, enjoying potato chips and tea, listening to mainland China shortwave radio, and scanning Weibo through a satellite connection. The SDF only has a limited number of Chinese linguists, so we can use all the help we can get. If the Ground Staff Office had anticipated this situation twenty years ago we could have poured more funding into properly training up Chinese linguists. So there's no problem?"

"Well, sir, if you've requested it, and she's okay with it, then who am I to say no?"

"Anyway, you should also prepare for evacuation while doing what you need to do. Nobody has the ability to stop the barrage of ballistic missiles from the mainland. Not even the U.S. military. All we can do is hope they direct the brunt towards Taiwan. The fewer the missiles, the higher our chances of intercepting them."

"Understood, sir. First, I'll change clothes." Harada's backpack and rifle were already prepared, along with his FAST helmet. He took them and left the room.

Domon glanced at the muted television. NHK was broadcasting information about the mainland obtained through amateur radio. From Hokkaido to Kyushu, the entire country was out of power. The water supply was functioning, but town gas was out everywhere.

2

Momentum

Commander Song Qin, leader of the PLA's Jiaolong Assault Team, retreated towards Ningbo-Zhoushan Naval Base on the captured MSDF air-cushioned landing craft. His platoon-sized unit that had landed was reduced to a third of its original size. He knew it would be a severe mission, but couldn't help but feel responsible for the outcome.

The PLA's attempt to occupy Diaoyu Island may have been a failure, but his small unit's capture of the enemy vessel was cause for accolades. Should they manage to survive this war, every member would probably be decorated with medals.

After handing temporary command of his unit to a subordinate, Commander Song boarded a helicopter that had come to pick him up, and flew to Ningbo-Zhoushan Naval Base. Prior to their deployment they had been repeatedly warned about MERS — Middle East Respiratory Syndrome and equipped with medical masks and disinfecting alcohol spray. He had heard that there had been cases of infection in Zhoushan.

Song disembarked from the helicopter at the naval base and was made to walk by himself to the apron. He didn't know where he was supposed to go, and was confused that no one was there to greet him. He sensed this place was different from other airfields. There were no fighter jets, and only a small number of patrol planes were parked on the tarmac. It wasn't a base buzzing with aircraft constantly taking off and landing; rather, it felt more like a logistics hub or rear training facility. When he tried to approach someone to ask questions, a soldier aimed his gun at him and warned, "Don't come any closer!"

Before long a young soldier brought him a folding chair and bottle of water and told him to sit there and wait. He figured that if someone had summoned him, they would come looking for him eventually. In the end, he was made to wait there for four hours. For the last three of those hours, he had his mask off, used his backpack as a pillow, and lay down on the ground to pass the time. The sound of aircraft taking off and landing woke him occasionally, but he would nod back off without too much care. His fatigue had accumulated from the intense combat he had endured.

No matter how many times they attacked, the enemy had forced them back. On such a small island, the enemy's forces should have been inferior to theirs, yet they failed to capture it. If this is how it was against the Japanese, he wondered, could they truly succeed against Taiwan with military force alone?

Finally hearing footsteps, Song turned his head to look in that direction. At first he couldn't make out who it was because of the mask the figure was wearing, but the presence of an aide-de-camp made him realise that this person was the very one who had brought him back from his scholarly pursuits at Peking University to the battlefield.

"What are you doing sleeping in a place like this?" asked Rear Admiral Ren Siyuan, who had dual roles as Director of the PLA Special Operations Division in the Joint Staff Department's Operations Bureau and Commander of Special Warfare Command.

"They put me here to prevent me getting infected. A base precaution."

"Rude bastards. Have you eaten?"

The commander shook his head and stood up. The admiral took a small folding chair from his aide-de-camp and ordered him to get some coffee.

"I'm sorry. I was able to arrange a plane for myself right away, but it took me some time to leave the Western Hills Command Center caves. There are already infected individuals in there. We have to get PCR tested every six hours."

"They haven't been able to stop the spread?"

"I guess not."

Commander Song put his mask back on and sat on the folding chair. The two of them sat face-to-face, three metres apart.

"First of all, well done on a hard job. It wasn't really our mission or responsibility, and it was a brutal operating environment."

"It was you who sent the *Turtle*, wasn't it, sir?"

"Yes, it was. I wasn't sure if it would be necessary, but I thought it would be better to launch it now rather than regret it later."

"What I don't get is why you didn't give us clear orders to use it?"

"The submersible commando function? I never imagined the situation would get so critical. When I first discovered that this thing was being developed, I asked that it be equipped to carry personnel. But they hadn't done any crewed underwater tests. The choice to use it or not, given the risks, was something I intended to leave to you, the on-the-ground commander. I'm relieved you managed to escape. The leadership in Zhongnanhai and the upper echelons of the PLAN are wringing their hands over how to rectify this crisis, but your men's capture and triumphant return of the air-cushioned landing craft blew all those worries away.”

“But we didn’t win. Couldn’t capture the island? Close to two companies’ worth of soldiers lost at sea without even reaching the island? And the two companies that did land reduced to a third. What was it? Six-hundred soldiers? Seven-hundred? All KIA for a deserted island. With the result being defeat…”

“Well, yes. If we fight like that during the Taiwan invasion, we’ll lose before it even becomes a question of whose responsibility. The leadership would inevitably have to bear that responsibility themselves.”

“Taiwan invasion? I thought we’d be done with that idea now?”

“If we miss this chance now, retaking Taiwan will become impossible. Right now is our chance, at the peak of our economic and military power. I’m not opposed to the idea in itself.”

“My team was almost entirely wiped out, but our next mission is to take Kinmen or the Matsu Islands?”

“I think that’s been considered, but it seems the higher-ups have finally woken up to the difficulties faced at Diaoyu Island. If we were to attack Kinmen or Matsu, small islands close to the mainland, the casualties would far exceed those at Diaoyu. If there ever was such a wasteful strategy, it seems it’s now been decided that the entire force should be directed to the conquest of Taiwan’s main island. In any case, your unit has reached its fighting limit and your troops need rest. And you’ve been assigned a mission suited to you alone. I want you to go to Japan. This war might drag on or it might end quickly. Either way, the key is to prevent Japan from interfering early on.”

“Is that the reason for the blackout? I hope it’s effective. Is it true that both the internet and mobile networks are down?”

"Yes. Except for Okinawa, Japan is entirely blacked out. We can't even contact our operatives there. We can only send one-way orders and messages of encouragement via encrypted short-wave radio. We prepared for as much, but there isn't anyone who can organise the units on the ground there. Japan will restore power and transport soon enough, but we'll need to continue our destabilisation efforts. For that purpose, we have to send in a commander trained in the field."

"I understand. But I can't just enter the country via Haneda or Kansai Airports now, can I? Don't tell me I'll be airlifted near some Kyushu beach and made to row a boat the rest of the way?"

"There is a way…" said the Rear Admiral Ren with a sly smile. "The high-ranking SDF officers that you brought back, including the general, will be returned to Japan today, or maybe tomorrow morning at the latest."

"Really? Without interrogating them?"

"If they had any strategic decision-making authority it would be a different story, but at this stage trying to extract tactical information on the Amphibious Rapid Deployment Brigade is pretty pointless. If we were to interrogate them for information, we're looking at a minimum six months just to build rapport. Japan has already returned our pilots who were downed over the Diaoyus via the Russians. We decided to follow suit and return their POWs the same day. We got Russia to mediate. That's the underlying reason. We thought this would go smoothly, but for some reason the Japanese hesitated…They said it was impossible to receive them because the blackout is preventing the use of airport navigation aids."

"Ah, I see. Organisations during these times are painful wherever you go. If this was the other way round and they were high-ranking Chinese POWs coming back, they'd be thrown into some prison in Tibet or somewhere as a warning to their local units. But they can't do that in Japan. The police hold far more power there than the military — the Self-Defense Forces. So, as soon as they land somewhere in Japan, they'll be interrogated by the public security authorities in the police, not the military police. They'll be relentlessly interrogated for three days and nights, exhaustively questioned about non-existent collusion with enemy contacts, and once completely worn out, handed back to the SDF. In their state of exhaustion, someone will put a pistol on a table and say, 'I'm misplacing this pistol here. There's a bullet inside. You decide.'"

"Indeed. And in doing so, naturally, it will rattle the frontline troops. That's the difference between a military like ours, accustomed to political purges and prepared for that kind of thing from the start, and a democratic country like Japan. Anyway, we want to send them back as quickly as possible as a psychological tactic. We managed to get the Japanese government to agree to a visual landing at Niigata Airport. The navaids aren't operational, but they're heading there on a Russian civilian plane. You'll land at Niigata with a Russian diplomatic passport. You and the prisoners will fly separately to Harbin before that, and there you'll hide at the back of the passenger plane to avoid being seen. You'll be met at the Russian Embassy in Tokyo. Russia has agreed to that much.

"Our covert operations units have been getting support from Japanese radicalist groups. Care has been taken to ensure no connections are made off to the side, as, naturally, those types of groups are monitored by security agencies there. Japan's become quite a surveillance society in recent times. We believe a significant portion of our units were exposed at the start of our campaign."

The admiral's aide-de-camp brought in a pot of coffee, paper cups and some biscuits.

"How'd you go with food over there?"

"Not bad. We slaughtered some mountain goats that had been bred on the island and cooked them up. After that, the nutritional jelly that you sent could have done with a bit more flavour, sir. Nutritional value aside, we held our noses and sucked it down."

"Ah, honestly, I wouldn't be brave enough to try it…unless I was stranded on a deserted island and had endured hunger for three days and three nights." The admiral sipped at his coffee then signalled to his aide-de-camp to place a briefcase between himself and the commander. It was the kind of item one would expect a diplomat to carry.

"You'll get a suit and leather shoes later. In here are two bundles of thousand yen notes and three bundles of ten-thousand yen notes. If that's not enough you can get more funding in-country. There's also a minimal amount of clothes and socks, as well as a smartphone charger. You'll be able to use the smartphone when the mobile network is restored, but choose the locations where you use it carefully. You'll be tracked. The portable battery can be used as a charger of course, but the top of it has been modified to function as a satellite communication antenna — sending and receiving text data only though. If you submerge it in water, a safety circuit triggers the lithium-ion battery to ignite, destroying anything and everything. There's a document in there that explains how to use these items. Read it, remember it, destroy it. On the smartphone there's a file with a list of all the operatives under your command and details on how to contact them. The code is your service number minus one. You get three attempts then the lithium-ion battery in the phone ignites."

"I thought I was leaving my military service behind…"

"Well, consider it a sightseeing trip to Tokyo. Honestly, there's still debate over whether Japan will enter the war. What do you think?"

"For Japan, Diaoyu Island was, in one way or another, a matter of national territorial defence. With the U.S. hesitating, whether or not Japan would expressly participate in a Chinese civil conflict is the question. The new Japanese prime minister is pragmatic and not inclined towards narrow-minded nationalism, and the factions that do want to participate are having a hard time convincing him. They may see him as a villain to assassinate."

"I don't think so. Japan isn't the kind of country that would change its national or organisational mindset just because its top leader changes."

"Fair enough."

A white-painted business jet came in for landing.

"You'll take that to Harbin. Apparently it was confiscated from some real estate mogul and is fitted out with a shower and double bed. At least shave before you go. I have a meeting here later with a staff officer from the East Sea Fleet."

"Well then, sir, I pray for success in the conquest of Taiwan," said Commander Song as he stood and saluted.

"Yes. If we reunite with Taiwan, 'The Chinese Dream' will be realised. Then this military expansion can end, and we'll be out of a job. You won't ever have to put on your boots again and can devote yourself to your beloved Japanese studies."

"Let's hope so, sir."

He took the briefcase then this time a car came to pick him up and dropped him off near the runway. He started running towards the business jet making a U-turn at the end of the runway.

Rear Admiral Ren Siyuan sat back down on the folding chair and watched as the business jet carrying Commander Song

Qin took off. He guessed it would probably leave Harbin after midnight and arrive at Niigata Airport by dawn tomorrow.

A patrol helicopter flew in from the sea and landed on a distant apron. It dropped off a naval officer dressed in coveralls, then flew to the opposite side of the runway. The naval officer gestured to him.

"Inconsiderate bunch…" grumbled Ren as he began to walk. But the man didn't come to greet him; instead, he walked towards the hangar on his own accord. Numerous night encampment tents were set up by the hangar.

A carrier-based early warning aircraft and a four-engine large patrol aircraft were parked in front of the hangar. Ren could see they were testbed platforms. The men entered the hangar without hesitation. A huge table was spread out inside, cluttered with computers, monitors, and blueprints.

"Sincerest apologies, Admiral, sir. I'm Senior Captain Ma Qinglin, East Sea Fleet staff officer. I heard you've gone out of your way to be here. Thank you for making time in your schedule." Senior Captain Ma had removed his mask briefly to make the introduction, but his apology lacked an air of sincerity. Ren gathered from the expression on Ma's face that he wanted to have a frank discussion as two colleagues in positions of responsibility.

"Sir, please allow me to introduce two female engineers making breakthroughs for our future force. This is Commander Hao Fei, responsible for developing the dual-band radar for the KJ-600, and Lieutenant Commander Zhong Guilan, responsible for the light detection and ranging system on the Y-9X patrol aircraft. And this individual here with no rank, looking rather like a new recruit, is Dr. Zhang Gaoyuan, a brilliant mathematician from the S Agency. Dr. Zhang and Lieutenant Commander Zhong were shot down just after discovering a Japanese submarine with the LiDAR system, and had to spend a harrowing night at sea until a Japanese patrol boat rescued them. Soon after they thought they were safe, a Japanese submarine mistook the patrol boat for one of ours and sank it, forcing them to drift again until finally being saved by a Japanese flying boat and repatriated through some backchannel negotiations. They went through it all and barely escaped with their lives. Commander Hao Fei, too, had a narrow escape after her plane was targeted by an Aegis fire control radar when it had flown forward a little too far. They managed to evade just as the system launched. All of them are seasoned heroes."

"A genius from the S Agency, huh…" To Ren he looked more like a kid. The harsh drifting must have changed his appearance. His eyes were still slightly bloodshot.

"Did you hear about the engagements two days ago?" asked Ma.

"No, I haven't. There's been a gag order on that. I've only heard that it was a large-scale attack by a joint U.S.-Japan force, with several fighters shot down and one or two warships possibly sunk. I don't know how the Taiwanese are reporting it. Your presence here suggests that our carrier strike group hasn't been completely wiped out."

"To be precise, just four manned fighters and two unmanned combat air vehicles wiped out two of our fighter squadrons before we even committed. And during the fight, likely another two stealth UCAVs easily penetrated our fleet's air defences and sank two supply ships and two frigates. One of the sunk frigates was just five kilometres away from one of our carriers. It was like shooting fish in a barrel, as the Americans would say."

"These four fighters, were they stealth fighters? F-22s perhaps?"

"No, they were F-15s. Of course they appeared on radar. But they were the latest variant, carrying up to sixteen air-to-air missiles. Commander Hao, show the good admiral the data."

The senior captain showed Ren the chilling data on an external monitor.

"Our KJ-600's dual-band radar can detect the enemy's F-35 stealth fighter. Initially, four F-15 Eagles and four F/A-18 Super Hornets appeared, so we suspected they were decoys and that the real players — F-35s — were lurking nearby. But we soon assessed that the F/A-18s were actually EA-18G Growler electronic attack aircraft. We suffered some heavy jamming and the scopes went all white, as you can see here. They were using barrage jamming techniques, so a wide range of frequencies were jammed. Our guys were getting seriously jammed; meanwhile, the enemy launched XQ-58 Valkyrie UCAVs in advance, and the Eagles used their optical sensors to find us and fire their AMRAAMs."

"I don't know my missiles well enough. AMRAAM is radar guided, unlike the Sidewinder, right?"

"Affirmative, it stands for Advanced Medium-Range Air-to-Air Missile. But it can be launched towards the calculated intercept point using optical sensors. The AMRAAM only uses its radar in the last part of the engagement sequence. With only this capability, four enemy fighters shot down forty of ours. And while our eyes were blinded by the barrage jamming, two UCAVs snuck into the airspace above our fleet and sank two supply ships and two frigates. Needless to say, had the Americans felt so inclined, they would have sunk our carrier as well. They absolutely could have. But they chose to sink the nearby frigates instead, probably just to demonstrate their capability."

"Does this mean the UCAV's missiles are stealth as well?"

"We were attacked while under barrage jamming, so it's still unclear what kind of missiles the UCAVs employed. If we analyse the data in detail, it's possible that there are radar waves emitted by the missiles hidden in the gaps between the jamming signals. In any case, the fact is no one noticed these small, stealthy drones pushing right in close to us. And we weren't just using radar; of course we were also monitoring the airspace with infrared sensors, but that didn't stop them slipping through." Senior Captain Ma continued, "Those stealth aircraft probably flew in at low altitude, skimming along the surface of the ocean. When they fly very low, even infrared sensors can be deceived. The air just above the surface of the ocean does have a relatively high humidity, not quite the density of steam though."

"How many fighters and ships have we lost in these battles over these last two weeks up to now?"

"Still under ten ships. That's excluding the five coast guard ships sunk by the Taiwanese at the onset of the conflict. Three were killed by Japanese submarines. As for fighter jets, we've probably lost around three-hundred of the relatively newer models, along with the highly skilled pilots. Likely eight in ten pilots in the fighters that were shot down didn't survive. In contrast, the total number of enemy fighters we've shot down, combining both Japanese and Taiwanese forces, doesn't even reach twenty. We were more than decimated.

"It's not entirely bleak, though. Thanks to Dr. Zhang's efforts, the patrol aircraft's LiDAR is starting to show results. The Japan Maritime Self-Defense Force's subs can no longer navigate freely in the waters of the continental shelf. And Commander Hao's KJ-600 airborne early warning aircraft can see the enemy's stealth fighters. Unfortunately, we only have one of each fully operational. Commander Hao, do we have any countermeasures against their barrage jamming?"

"We're still looking into it, sir. But even if we come up with countermeasures, the U.S. will likely come at us with new tactics. It might be better to place more emphasis on detection with optical sensors. Both my aircraft and Lieutenant Commander Zhong's are equipped with such sensors."

"If only they can be integrated into the system in real-time and allow our jets to intercept…"

"Indeed. We'll continue to work on it."

"Please do so. Dr. Zhang, let's talk later. The Navy can never thank you enough for your contributions and the dangers you've faced. I've spoken to the S Agency about giving you an appropriate position after this war is over."

"I don't need a position; please just make it possible for me to attend academic conferences abroad. I'm like a bird in a cage here. I want you to remember that I could have applied for asylum in Japan if I'd wanted to."

"I understand. You've proven your loyalty. Let's discuss that as well later on."

Senior Captain Ma cleared the room, sat down to face Rear Admiral Ren, and removed his mask. "I'm sick of these things. Is there any chance at all that you could be infected, sir?"

"Don't think so." The admiral also removed his mask and placed it on the desk. "With this thing on, I can't read expressions or convey the nuances of my words."

"Frankly, I'm starting to doubt whether the leadership in Beijing truly understands the situation on the ground. This is a flaw of our system. Secrecy is rampant. The right hand doesn't know what the left is doing."

"Well, I'm afraid not even I can grasp what's happening in Zhongnanhai, and I'm based at the *Caves* in Western Hills. The Navy's higher-ups must surely be aware of the sacrifices made."

"Sir, if they were aware, this war would have been over by now. The Diaoyu Island operation was supposed to be over the day after the landing...U.S. Forces are one thing, but we even struggled against the Japanese. We launched several saturation attacks with land attack missiles targeting their troops dug in on the west side of the island, but not a single one hit. And they only needed one Aegis ship at a time to shoot down every one of our missiles. They possessed combat capabilities of another dimension. They're a formidable adversary."

"How much of our combat power have we lost, I wonder?"

"In terms of surface ships, it's not too bad since we were hunkered down along the coast. Mostly a decrease in morale. The three aircraft carriers are also unscathed. The problem lies with our air power. At the very least, a quarter of the Navy and Air Force's fighters, probably a third of our combat strength, must have been lost. Although, we probably still outnumber the Japanese and Taiwanese forces in terms of total number of fighters..."

"There's no way around it. At least one million ground troops will be needed to take control of the island of Taiwan. And we'd need China's entire maritime transport capability to maintain logistics. And yet, the Army believes that landing a force of a mere hundred thousand will make the Taiwan Presidential Office fold and surrender. And if it doesn't, they think if it comes to a war of attrition, we'd have the upper hand."

"Our outlook was overly optimistic for the Pratas Islands as well. With such an optimistic view, we were doomed at Diaoyu Island, and we'll face the same fate with Taiwan."

"Once a campaign is set in motion, it can't be stopped..."

"What's your next move, sir?"

"I'm reorganising the Navy landing force to get maximum results with minimum strength. All we have to do then is pray that the Navy can control the Strait and maintain logistics without interruption. Both Vice Admiral Tang Dongming of the East Sea Fleet and Vice Admiral Dong Xiaoning of the South Sea Fleet are excellent commanders; I'm not worried about that aspect. Even an amateur like myself understands that losing air superiority means the end of this war. The key question is whether America will get involved, isn't it?"

"Indeed, but that's beyond our control. The government is probably negotiating with the American interlocutors. So far, the Americans have supported Japan and Taiwan at critical moments. If they keep supporting the war effort like this, even without their full involvement, our losses will continue to mount."

"I understand the situation, but what am I to do?"

"You appear to have some backers in Zhongnanhai."

"No, no, it's not like that. My unit is only appreciated for its utility. We failed in our attacks against every ship, and we can't say we achieved any sort of success on Diaoyu Island."

"Even Japan could single handedly sink a carrier. Taiwan could too, if they're prepared to take the losses. Back in the day when I was living in America, I was told repeatedly by Americans that Chinese people can adapt; that this was China's strength. That Japanese people can't adapt; that they are a people who see no value in adapting. But if I dare point out a flaw in we Chinese, it's that once we're in momentum, we can't stop. Even if we realise we've taken the wrong course, we tend to just push on through until we meet with catastrophe. That's the weakness of a totalitarian system like communism. And we're riding this momentum right at this moment. I only pray that what awaits us is victory and not a sheer cliff."

"It's going to be tough. The 'momentum' you're talking about didn't just start yesterday or today. This dangerous drive has been underway for many years already."

"That's how I see it, sir," said the senior captain, nodding his head.

The seed was sewn by the previous generation, Ma thought, and we're paying for their grandiloquent words about national prestige and the Chinese Dream with the lives of our young soldiers, sailors and airmen. No one inside China, no one in the world can stop it. Not even America can stop it. No one will even try. We grasped hegemony, scowled at the world, and threatened it at every turn, and this is the result.

Futoshi Tanaka, the former GSDF master sergeant and sales team member at the Hachioji Center in the western outskirts of Tokyo, had split up his task with his colleague and had made the rounds through nearly thirty convenience stores in Hachioji. Their area of responsibility went beyond Hachioji and included Hinohara Town and Otsuki City to the west. They had to cover and back up close to one-hundred stores. These days there were twice as many convenience stores as post offices. They had to provide support to stores of rival companies as well.

At the request of the police, Tanaka went to post some information at a rival company's convenience store near the Takao Police Station. He took some empty shelves outside and placed fliers on them in tiers. Residents were coming and going, and the toilets were still mostly functioning there. The water supply facilities were still operational, but there had been warnings that this was expected to change before long.

Even though the supplies he provided, such as printing paper, contributed a mere drop in the ocean, his efforts nonetheless brought a sense of encouragement to the young part-timers and housewives at the store. At this store too, paper with TOKYO

TOWER 20:00 had been printed out. When the store manager inquired about its meaning, Tanaka deflected with a non-committal, "Who knows...?"

Tokyo Tower had never been visible from here at Hachioji, but one could catch a glimpse of it a few kilometres further west atop Mt. Takao on a clear day. It was forty kilometres from Tokyo Tower to Mt. Takao, about the distance that Tanaka had travelled just today.

Riding a bicycle all day was a literal pain in the backside. And there was a definite shortage of staff. The Hachioji Supply Depot still had supplies, but delivery vehicles were limited and the roads were congested, so he had to complete his mission through sheer grind. Hopefully someone was sorting something out with the Hachioji Ward Office.

Just as Tanaka went to leave this store, he collided with a huge man wearing a convenience store apron. As he stumbled, he looked up at the man's face.

"Ah, Mr. Tanaka! How long has it been!"

Standing at nearly six-foot three, Yusuke Shimoyama was a giant of a man who Tanaka had remembered had played university football. During those days he had taken a part-time job at a nearby convenience store and quickly showed an ability to learn fast which led him to take on additional shifts at other stores. He was highly valued by the company as an emergency staff member. Although convenience stores often employ many part-timers, these employees frequently took time off. Shimoyama became the go-to person, dispatched with just a phone call to support stores in need of staff. Tanaka stepped outside and motioned for Shimoyama to follow him into a quiet spot.

"Shimoyama, I thought you'd started working full-time somewhere?"

"Ah, the company that gave me the formal offer went under when COVID hit. It was over before I'd even worked a day. I went back to my family in Nagoya for a while, but then came back to Tokyo again to try and find work. I've been crashing at my friend's place. Given what's going on, I thought the stores would be struggling, so I showed up, thinking there'd be nothing to sell. But there's still been a tonne of work to be done, so they asked me to help out."

"That's a big help! But why didn't you apply to our company after your job offer fell through?"

"I thought about my parents, and figured I could find work in Nagoya."

"Well, I can't promise anything, but you have useful skills, so if you like I can put in a good word and have you come and work for us? You might be put on a contract at first, but you'll be getting a wage, and we won't mind if you continue searching for full-time work. And it's not like your parents will get old any time soon. You can work here for a good four or five years."

"That would really help if you could do that for me. Honestly, since I'm already treated as a postgraduate, it's tough to fit into the new graduate slots."

"That being said, you have the physical strength; you'd be great for our logistics unit."

"That would be great! And this is a real surprise. Before I even got here, there were already notices up on the university campus telling people things like where sanitary products were available or how to get the latest government info."

"That's right. There was a plan in place that took a bit of time, aiming to turn convenience stores into logistics hubs during a blackout."

Several phone charging cables stretched out from power sockets outside the convenience store. Although the mobile phone service was still down, people could charge their phones for thirty minutes via an uninterrupted power supply device connected directly to solar panels. Around ten young people were sitting in the bicycle parking area. Under normal circumstances, these young people would be glued to their phones. Now, unable to do so, they stared blankly into space.

About fifty people came in and out of the store while Tanaka was there. It felt similar to the hustle and bustle inside a convenience store during a summer fireworks festival. Only now there was basically nothing to sell. Milk had been kept behind the counter, given free of charge to mothers with small children, but it was almost gone after only thirty minutes.

"By the way, what's all this about Tokyo Tower? Even the store manager says he doesn't know…"

"Oh, it's nothing major. You can't see Tokyo Tower from here anyway, so knowing about it doesn't really matter," Tanaka explained in a low voice.

"It'd be good to go somewhere where we can see it. I'm pretty sure it's visible half-way up Mt. Takao."

"Didn't you used to run up it in your school days? But I guess you wouldn't want to go up there in these circumstances, and at night in the dark." Tanaka spoke with a slight chuckle. He often climbed Mt. Takao to maintain his own fitness. He wouldn't call hiking a pastime of his, but keeping fit was a habit he'd maintained from his time in the Self-Defense Forces.

"The Kompira-dai Trail is pretty quick, isn't it?"

"No, no, that trail is dark and too risky, even with a headlamp. But if you are going to climb it, take the easier and safer option up Trail One to the observatory. A fit fellow like you could do it in thirty minutes."

"Do you mind if I head back to university in a bit? I'll invite some of the juniors."

"Really? Well, sure. They'll need flashlights and water bottles. Don't forget to add salt. I'll come along with you. Even with my legs we'll be up and down in two hours. We'll drop by one of the stores on the way." It was already dusk. "Ninety minutes will give us plenty of time. We'll leave here at six thirty."

"Roger. In tough times like these, this will be a good memory for everyone." The young man removed his apron and handed it to Tanaka for safe keeping, then dashed out.

When Tanaka first heard about the Tokyo Tower idea, he wondered why they were allocating resources to something so pointless. What on earth were the higher-ups thinking...?

———

The dusk was settling over the Prime Minister's Office. Due to a malfunction in the generator, the entire building was embarrassingly still without electricity. Without power, the underground Crisis Management Centre remained shut. This was beyond unexpected. The only available toilet was in a government building accessible only by a tunnel. The cigar-loving prime minister had tried his best to hold back, but was now puffing down cigars without remorse. Thick cigar smoke wafted down from the Prime Minister's Executive Office on the fifth floor, filling the building with a smoky haze.

Prime Minister Shiro Aso descended to the fourth floor conference room. Everyone stood as he entered. He took his seat. "Well, have we come to a consensus?"

The Chief Cabinet Secretary shook his head. Sitting across from the Chief Cabinet Secretary was Hiroshi Kuwabara, Parliamentary Vice-Minister of Defense.

LED lanterns had been placed in each of the four corners of the room and four more were on the table which was draped in a white tablecloth. They cast an eerie glow. Despite being LED, the lights were made to flicker like flames, giving the impression of real lanterns. They were actually for camping. The light was dim and seemed to symbolise the state of the Japanese government at that moment.

"Who the hell are you? I can't see your face."

"Why, sir, I'm a Parliamentary Vice-Minister of Defense, appointed by the previous administration. I'm also a member of the National Defense Division, and a core member of the Japan-Taiwan Parliamentary Friendship Association. And I'm a member of your faction, Prime Minister."

"Ah, yes. But you know people in my faction are only after my money."

"That's not the case at all. Everyone is drawn to you because of your character, Prime Minister."

"Come to think of it, you're the politician who pestered Domon, threatening him over your son on the cruise ship, right?"

"Yes. I do regret my actions, but I am not ashamed. It was what I had to do as a father."

"Well, you're a good man. If I had to act for every bastard child of mine, I wouldn't have any stamina left in me. But you, of all people, shouldn't have known about that unit. Who told you?" The prime minister glared at the Chief of the Ground Self-Defense Force.

"Sir, I don't know anything about that," said General Yasuo Ushijima, sitting upright.

"Prime Minister, I'm not in the National Defense Division for nothing," said Kuwabara.

"The hardline National Defence Division…More like dorks than hawks, wouldn't you say? Bunch of fools."

"More importantly, sir, is it okay that we have an American here with us?"

Seated on a tablet arm chair at the end of the room, a step down from the main table and beside the back window, was a Caucasian man. His height, taller than the average Japanese, made him particularly conspicuous.

"Who are you? Who do you work for?" asked Aso.

"My name is Joe Stratton, Your Excellency. I am Counsellor for Government Affairs at the U.S. Embassy." The American responded in perfect Japanese followed by a bow.

"Okay, no problem. Whatever we discuss here will be transcribed within an hour and passed from our North American Affairs Division to your Empire. I don't mind. Or did you come here with some kind of request from your government?"

"No, sir. Today, I am here purely in the capacity of an observer, invited solely to listen. I consider myself without any authority to speak, and of course, I am not in a position to represent the views of the Department of Defense."

"Fine. I don't see any problems. How about you, Katakura?"

"No issues, sir. It was my decision to invite him," said Senior Deputy Minister for Foreign Affairs Soichiro Katakura from his seat beside the Chief Cabinet Secretary.

"Fine. So does the Ministry of Defense have power?"

"Yes, the building has its own power generator," said Kuwabara. "But to conserve power they've been cutting the lights in some places. The atmosphere isn't too much different from here."

"We ought to move over there. Come to think of it, they'd all shoot me daggers any time I lit up a cigar. But why shouldn't I be allowed to enjoy a cigar at my age? Anyway, what are you all thinking?"

"Sir, we must commit to full-scale military support for Taiwan!" Kuwabara asserted, his right hand clenched tightly on the table."

"Is this also the consensus of the uniformed members here?"

As well as the Chief of Staff of the GSDF, the Chiefs of Staff of the Air and Maritime Self-Defense Forces were also present. Standing silent behind them were a number of other uniformed personnel, about ten in total. A group of high-ranking officials from the Ministry of Foreign Affairs sat on the other side of the table.

"Sir, we Chiefs of Staff will refrain from asserting our opinions on the matter," said the Chief of the GSDF. "This venue is too politically charged for us to comment. That is our consensus."

"Is this a *perilous situation around Japan*? Is it constitutional to continue the defence mobilisation order?"

"We have assurances from the Cabinet Legislation Bureau. War in Taiwan is absolutely a *perilous situation around Japan*, and deploying the SDF for Taiwan's defence is completely constitutional!" Kuwabara stated emphatically.

"That can't be right. Taiwan is considered Chinese territory, isn't it? If that's the case, what we have occurring here is a civil conflict, no? So how is meddling in a civil conflict in any way constitutional?"

"Prime Minister, the nature of this situation is fundamentally different to Hong Kong."

"How so? It's exactly the same as Hong Kong. Taiwan might have had an autonomous government, but the central government in Beijing is just trying to oust them because they don't like their bad attitude. And the argument that Taiwan is highly democratic doesn't hold either. If it did, the Empire would have gone in by now. Isn't that right, Mister?" Aso turned to address Joe Stratton. "You understand what I mean by 'the Empire'?"

"Of course, sir. I've heard it's a term of reference for American imperialism, a term radicals used in the past to criticise the U.S.

The meaning is a little…outside the bounds of what a diplomat would comment on…"

"Correct. If Taiwan's highly democratic system was something worth protecting for the West, the Empire would have intervened already, but it hasn't. There's the Taiwan Relations Act between America and Taiwan which absolutely allows for military cooperation, right? Despite that, the Empire still hasn't made a move! So why should Japan, which doesn't even have formal diplomatic relations with Taiwan, let alone a military alliance, poke its head into a Chinese civil war and spill blood? Bit odd, isn't it?"

"What will you do about semiconductors, Prime Minister?" asked Kuwabara. "If China gains control over Taiwan's semiconductor plants, our entire industrial base will be at their mercy."

"Why not just buy them from Communist China? Whether the semiconductors are painted red or not, as long as they work as semiconductors then what does it matter? Just because China takes the lead in the semiconductor industry, doesn't mean they won't sell them to us. What's the Ministry of Foreign Affairs' take on this?" The prime minister turned to Katakura for an answer.

"This is our analysis. If the U.S. does not participate in the war and Japan alone backs Taiwan by fighting, and should we be successful and China backs down, the U.S. will quickly mend its relations with China, and the economic relationship between them will deepen as if nothing ever happened. But not only would the lives of the SDF personnel have been lost, China would then likely launch severe economic retaliation against us. Conversely, if Japan were to support Taiwan alone, and Taiwan regretfully surrenders, the sacrifices of our personnel would have been in vain, and the security of our petroleum supply routes would be under constant threat, leading to a future where we face daily confrontations with the PLA Navy around the Ryukyu Islands. To sum, from MOFA's perspective, we assess that Japan's involvement without the U.S. brings excessively high risk whether we win or lose."

"I concur. Then it's decided." Aso went to stand up, but Kuwabara did so first in an attempt to reason with him.

"Prime Minister, please! Just a moment! This is very one-sided. And I cannot accept that I'm the only one here in support of defending Taiwan!"

"Well, objectively speaking, it just doesn't make sense for Japan to participate. I just cannot agree with such a reckless proposal. Are you saying we should abandon a market of 1.4 billion people just to save twenty million Chinese who have tasted a bit of freedom? Japan has come to rely on China for everything, right down to the last screw. And the fact that the Empire has decided to stay silent probably boils down to that, doesn't it? The time of American hegemony is well past its peak. Hegemony has shifted to China. I think we have nothing but to face this reality."

"If Taiwan falls we will be facing a situation far beyond mere confrontations over the Senkakus!"

"Even so, is it right to let SDF personnel die in defence of Taiwan? The Ground Chief of Staff is already in turmoil over a mere seventy casualties. How many thousands more will die in battle after this? The potential future threat to Okinawa doesn't justify such a cost."

The Chief Cabinet Secretary quietly signalled to Kuwabara to take a seat.

Joe Stratton felt like he was watching a debate back home, a discussion at the State Department on a slightly smaller scale. Even America now bought everything from China, down to the last screw. And for China, whether it was grain, beef, or aeroplanes, it was America's biggest customer. They couldn't easily afford to upset them. Seeing the discussion here, it made sense why America hadn't raised a hand to defend Taiwan. Regrettably, he too couldn't help but feel the era of American hegemony had come to an end.

3

Tokyo Tower

Female university student Minami Komatsu, who lived in the run-down apartment in Setagaya, was about to head out for her evening part-time shift when she suddenly faced a severe crisis. Since the power was out, she wasn't able to apply her makeup properly. It was still light outside, so she had to take her makeup compact over to the window side and use the natural light there to do herself up.

Fire engines and ward office public address vehicles were driving around blaring messages from their megaphones, but she couldn't catch what they were saying.

Figuring the shelves at the convenience store would be empty anyway, Minami thought she'd just show her face then be told to go home for the day. Maintaining goodwill was important. It wasn't like her hourly wage would increase because of it, but she was on good terms with the elderly couple who ran the store.

The proprietor husband had been hospitalised with cancer recently and his wife, the proprietress, had been struggling. Fortunately, it turned out to be a treatable form of cancer, and the surgery had gone well. Although her husband was still in the hospital, the proprietress seemed relieved now, but she was still running the store on her own. With part-timers coming and going, she was probably feeling quite alone, so Minami thought it important to at least drop by and offer some encouragement.

It would probably be completely dark by the time she headed back home later. She didn't have a proper flashlight, but six months ago a nerdy male student had gifted her a Mini Maglite. She recalled it was a prize from one of those claw machine games at an arcade. She had left it somewhere on her makeup shelf. It required a single AAA battery. When she turned it on, it shone as expected. The battery was still the original test item that had come with it, but it would suffice for her trip to the store and back. Besides, her bicycle was also equipped with a light.

Minami slipped into her sneakers in the dim light and opened the door, feeling a bit uneasy. She could still make out the wall of the neighbouring apartment building, although it was very dark. The darkness of her apartment had made her preparations take longer than usual. But, having decided to go, all that was left was to actually proceed. It wasn't as if she needed to catch a train. The store was a mere two kilometres away, in the opposite direction of the station.

Minami had deliberately sought out a convenience store that was somewhat removed from the nearest train station so she wouldn't encounter any neighbours. And she had chosen to work at a convenience store because she figured it would fit well with her university studies. The work was tough, but it was far better than door-to-door sales or the adult entertainment industry.

But the moment she left her apartment, she felt disheartened. She could still make out the outlines of houses. And looking up, she could see red rotating lights flickering here and there, probably patrol cars and fire engines on duty. She could also see the lights of bicycles, but there were hardly any private cars on the road. Every now and again, the figure of a person would appear.

"It's so dark…" she blurted out without thinking. Actually, it wasn't completely dark yet. But it was certainly dark enough. It reminded her of the time she went on a club retreat near Lake Kawaguchi. Minami hated darkness…It revived memories she had long sealed away, memories from a distant past.

She pedalled slowly. This area had always been safe. Setagaya was more of an old area of Tokyo than a wealthy one. It was getting darker, but she noticed that not all the lights were out. The lights were on in a convenience store up ahead. Out the front of the store stood a large, illuminated signboard. The light from it gently brightened the residential area outside.

Minami worried she might lose track of exactly where she was, something she was prone to doing at the best of times, but recalling the shop lights told her that she was on the right path. She passed by a group of students holding flashlights. They looked to be a group of six high school boys in uniform, walking with megaphones. They were broadcasting information, either government announcements or notices from the local ward office.

It was far easier to understand these announcements than the ones from the public address vehicles earlier. They were joking around as they walked. For Minami it was a moment of relief. She then came across a queue of people, although there was no gymnasium or community hall around here.

The store where she worked was located by a narrow creek. The queue of people formed along the promenade that ran alongside the creek. What was this? she thought, before realising the queue led to her own convenience store. It was the only illuminated building in the area. The store's five-metre-tall illuminated signboard also served as a street lamp, brightly lighting the surrounding area. More than two-hundred people were in a line outside the store waiting to charge their smartphones. Another line had also formed of people waiting for the arrival of new stock.

There was an entry restriction in place at the entrance of the store. Minami had never seen such a thing at a convenience store before. Given there probably wasn't much stock to begin with, she wondered what they were doing. All together there were probably four- or five-hundred people surrounding this small residential convenience store. Police had also arrived and were managing the traffic.

As it grew darker, it felt like more people were gathering. Since there was a promenade, there was space to disperse the crowd that had gathered. Minami regretted that she had come by bicycle. The parking area for storing rental electric bicycles was usually empty.

The convenience store was the only place lit up. The electric decorative signage, known in the industry as facade signage, made to wrap around the edge of the store's roof, was glowing brightly. But the interior of the store was dark.

With no other choice, Minami squeezed her bicycle through the crowd into the rental bicycle parking area and locked it. This store operated 24/7 and didn't have shutters. There was a back door, but it was hardly ever used. If she remembered correctly, there were cardboard boxes stacked up in front of it.

Minami pushed her way through and entered the store, which was also dark inside. Only two LED bulbs were on. In fact, it was brighter under the signboard street lamp outside. She apologised to her part-time coworkers for being late and asked where the proprietress was. Someone pointed towards the inside, to the office beyond the bathroom.

She entered the four-digit code into the electronic lock and entered the office. The proprietress was seated in a chair, her head resting on the table, asleep and softly snoring. A lamp on the desk glowed, set to night mode, casting a light as gentle as a candle. When the proprietress realised the door had opened, she raised her head, her expression ghostly.

"Are you okay, Ma'am?"

"Ah! Miss Minami! You're here! How is the store?"

"Umm…it's surrounded by a massive crowd of people! The shelves are totally empty. It's like there's been a disaster." A partly-consumed drink was on the table. A stimulant beverage. Half of it remained. "How long have you been working, Ma'am?"

"Since the morning before yesterday…I think. Zhwan was here last night as usual, but she became all feverish and when I measured her temperature, it was thirty-eight degrees, so I sent her home. The other part-timer didn't turn up and didn't contact me. I tried calling you in the middle of the night, but…"

"I'm so sorry! I was out with my friends last night, when I got home I crashed out without even having a shower. I think I had my phone on silent. Have you heard from your husband?"

"I haven't heard a thing. But it's not like he's in ICU or anything, and that big hospital has its own power generator, so I think he'll be fine. If anything, he's probably more worried about us here." The proprietress looked exhausted and drank the remainder of her drink. She went to stand up but stumbled.

"Ah, Ma'am, please don't overdo it. Go home, please. I can manage things here. Anyway, we can only use cash right now, and it's not like there are any utility bill payments needing to be processed."

"There's a tonne of work to be done. Faxes are pouring in from headquarters."

"Faxes? But aren't the phone lines down?"

"Well, apparently the stores have been set up as hub centres, and special fax lines were connected. So even if the phones don't work, the stores can still connect with headquarters through fax."

"So that's why there are posters stuck up around the place… They usually do that at the community halls, though."

"What was your major again, Minami?"

"Distribution economics…supermarkets. But Ma'am, you should be sleeping. I'll take care of everything. Let's make space here." There were more than enough cardboard boxes to make a makeshift bed. Stacking four or five of them would work fine. Cardboard boxes could be used in place of a blanket too.

"Would you mind taking care of things here?" said the proprietress, her eyes drowsy.

"It's no problem at all! Please get some rest. I'll make sure nothing disturbs you. Where's the fax?" The fax machine wasn't in its usual place.

"Ah, I couldn't keep coming back in here all the time, so I extended the cable and placed it behind the register. We've already gone through two reams of paper. They could have at least made it an internet connection, seeing as they had the funds to install a dedicated line."

"For sure…" Minami found a round potato chip packet to use as a makeshift pillow. "Sleep well, Ma'am."

"Thank you. Also, follow the instructions or orders that come by fax. Occasionally we get a message asking to search for a person. Make sure to follow those ones. They'll complain to us later if we don't."

"Searching for someone? What do you mean?"

"Like if there's a salaryman living nearby who has an elderly mother living alone in Osaka. He's worried because she's starting to become senile and he can't get in touch with her. He believes a convenience store nearby might help, so we send a fax to headquarters requesting someone to check on her and take her somewhere safe if need be. Then, headquarters would look up the address, find the closest affiliated store, and send the fax there. That store might then pass the fax to the local police or fire department. And if a safety check is done, the response would be faxed back to the headquarters, and from there, it gets sent out to someone who can deliver the message directly to the person concerned. Be prepared, we get these requests non-stop."

"Oh, I see. I'll be certain to keep an eye on those ones. Please rest now." Minami donned her convenience store apron and annotated her starting time on the board. Despite there being nothing left to sell, she thought about the challenge of handling such a large crowd of customers. She attached a name badge that read 'Kitamachi' to the left side of her chest. There was no particular origin for the name Kitamachi, but it served as a kind of talisman to ward off stalkers. It was also a rule here not to call the owners 'boss' in front of the customers. The owners, too, had aliases, as did everyone else. They liked to joke that these names were like *geisha* aliases.

Upon stepping behind the cash register counter, she found the youngest of her male part-time coworkers sorting through a pile of coins. "What time did your shift start, Yasu?" she asked. His name wasn't on the sign-in board earlier.

"Since yesterday morning. The time clock wasn't working."

"How long are you going to work for?"

"I've got the energy, so it's no problem at all. Ma'am is pretty tired…"

"She's sleeping on some cardboard boxes I laid out. Please make sure no one goes in there. Who's been in charge here?"

"Me. Everyone's pretty freaked out. Some of the part-timers have popped in, but headed back home soon after. I get why the housewife part-timers can't come in though. Including myself, there are five of us. It got a bit easier when the cops arrived to control the crowd. Right now we're just keeping watch of the phone charging area. Not sure why everyone's so obsessed with charging their phones. Not like there's any signal or anything."

Young Koji Yasu's name badge read 'Seta'. He had only just turned eighteen and had arrived as a high-school student to work part-time, but seemed prone to skipping classes, then dropped out of school to work almost full-time. The proprietress didn't look too kindly on this, preferring that he would attend school, but her husband welcomed him, suggesting that life wasn't all about school. Yasu wanted to save money quickly and start his own business.

"Well, I'll take over from here, you can be 2IC. Is there anything we need to get sorted right away?"

"A truck from the delivery centre came here four hours ago. We haven't received many things, they said it's because this store is in the middle of a residential neighbourhood. We got maybe ten small boxes' worth, and those were cleaned out in like ten minutes. A third of the people waiting couldn't come through. We got an earful of complaints."

Minami took out her Mini Maglite and shone it on the inside of the counter. The fax machine was churning out paper again. "Where are all the faxes from headquarters?"

Yasu opened a cardboard box that had been placed on the floor.

"Whoa, this many…?" There was a stack of what would normally be two months' worth of promotional faxes.

"I've been placing them in there in the order they arrived." Yasu picked up the stack of paper. "It's pretty weird. Whoever this Business Continuity Plan HQ chief is has stamped their name on every one of these papers. Then there's this 'Tokyo Tower 20:00'? It's written on the bottom of every page, but no one has any idea what it means."

"Give me a bit of time. I'll go through all of these. Also, could you please move the empty shelves and make a direct path to the bathroom? There's nothing on the shelves to sell, so make do with the table that's been taken outside the store. A bit like what we do during summer festivals. Now, if we make some space on this side, we'll have a place for us to rest. If a sick person were to come then we can move them there too."

Minami held the Mini Maglite between her lips and began checking through each of the pages atop the counter. The first page, written by the BCP headquarters chief in thick marker said, "Hang in there! Help is on its way!" Judging from the timestamp, it was sent just after the power went out last night. The BCP headquarters chief had stamped his signature on this one too, but there was no mention of Tokyo Tower.

The second page onwards was a crisis response manual. The company had prepared for such a contingency. A plan had been put together to utilise convenience stores as local disaster response centres, and they wanted everyone to lead these efforts. The subsequent pages provided detailed instructions, so if they followed this crisis response manual then there should be no issues. It stated that while it was unclear how long it would take for the crisis to be resolved, improved road conditions could allow for delivery operations to go ahead as normal or even more frequently, regardless of whether the electricity had been restored.

The manual was almost fifty pages long and detailed everything from making a megaphone from items available in the store, to the expansion of the stores' discretionary authority for the temporary employment of part-time workers, and how it wasn't necessary to stick to cash transactions.

A new fax even arrived while Minami was in the middle of reading them. It included the latest information about the delivery schedule, detailing the store names and approximate arrival times of delivery vehicles to each store. According to the schedule, a delivery vehicle should have arrived twenty minutes ago. There was no dedicated line linking the delivery vehicles to the delivery centre.

"Hey Yasu, do you think the night shift will come?"

"I don't think it's possible. Kudo is two stations away. She'd have to come by bicycle. And there's Kimura. He's skipped shift twice before without letting us know. He was warned if that happened again he's a goner. I don't think that guy will turn up at a time like now. Keiko has been on since the morning shift, but she's probably reaching her limits now. And besides, she still hasn't got the hang of it after a month on the job, and she's cried a bunch of times when customers have yelled at her."

"Well, let's start advertising for staff! It says right here on this piece of paper from BCP HQ not to hesitate in hiring staff on the spot if required, and to offer a daily wage. Does it mention settling payments in ways other than cash? Like, on account or something?"

"Ah, that…You mean if we're supposed to take down customers' point card numbers, or if their smartphone is on, note down their phone number and let them have the items on a tab, right? That's impossible with the staff we have. We're not even getting enough stuff in to cover the customers who pay in cash."

"In that case we'll hire part-timers specifically for that task. It says right here that for daily wages, all payments will be settled later and covered by headquarters."

"That's all good and well for stores that are next to train stations, but who in this fancy neighbourhood is going to put their hand up to work here?"

"We can only ask." Minami readied herself and stepped out from behind the cash register counter. The automatic doors at the entrance of the store had been left wide open of course. Carts and crates had been placed outside, ready for the delivery vehicles to take back. Oddly, there were even crates for bottled beer among them. They didn't sell such items here, so perhaps someone had brought them in to use as makeshift chairs.

Minami recalled what her uncle, a firefighter, had once said to her when she was little. "The day will come when you're going to have to help someone. The day will come when you will have to make sacrifices and dig deep for others. Study and learn every day for when that day arrives." That uncle never made it back… Nobody did, and on that day, her hometown vanished, leaving Minami suddenly all alone. For the past ten years she had lived with the memories of that day, that moment, sealed away.

Minami paused for a moment, rubbing the area around the pit of her stomach, then took a deep breath and stepped onto one of the overturned crates. "Excuse me everyone! I'm a student part-timer here. I've been here for eighteen months."

Someone in the dark at the back of the crowd shouted, "We can't hear you!"

A police officer offered her a small handheld megaphone to use. "Thank you, officer." She turned back to the crowd. "I have something to ask of you all. The owner of this store is suffering from cancer and can't be here. His wife is running the business, but she's been working non-stop for the last two days and she was close to collapse, so we have her resting in the office at the moment. While she's there, I'll be taking charge of things. But we're short on staff. I know it's a bit strange to think that we don't have enough staff even though there's nothing to sell, but we're going to try and put on some new part-time staff. We're looking for volunteers, and we will pay you a daily rate in cash at the end of each work day. If you have some way to prove your identity and an emergency contact, we're willing to hire you. Experience is welcome, but anyone with even a little customer service experience would be warmly received. We want to be able to sell items without cash, so we welcome people who know how to keep account books. We also need people who have experience designing posters, people who can write neatly, people who can illustrate, people who can manage the power generator. If you have any of those skills, please come forward. Your help would be greatly appreciated. We aim to keep serving until the lights come back on again and we want to keep this place lit as a beacon of hope for the community! Thank you for your attention!"

Everyone around her was silent. It was a real disappointment. She should have expected that such an appeal to the people who had gathered at this convenience store in this upper-class neighbourhood would be futile; especially under these circumstances. Minami returned the handheld megaphone to the police officer and stepped down from the beer crate.

But just then from the dark, the soft voice of a girl called out. "I…I'm a certified Level Two bookkeeper. At the moment I'm going to one of those commercial high schools and I'm studying hard for the Level One exam. I came here so I could study under the light. I'm happy to help you out?"

"Oh my goodness, yes! Oh…but you're underage…"

"I told my parents I'm here. And besides, I'll be eighteen in a month!"

Someone in the crowd chimed in, "A bit young I think!"

Another hand went up. "Umm…I'm a student at an animation school and I dabble in anime. If you're ok with *kawaii*-style illustrations, I'm pretty confident in my skills…"

"Thank you. That would be amazing. Is there anybody else? Even for just two or three hours. Even if it's just to manage the queue, that would still help us."

Two, three, then five people under the illuminated signboard raised their hands. It now seemed they would need to set up a dedicated counter to process them.

Soon after, a slight, elderly man stepped forward. "I'm a high-voltage electrical engineer. Of course, I also hold a valid First-Class Electrician licence. Can't say I've ever wired a convenience store before, but I've worked on supermarkets. I've been telling your part-timers to turn off the electricity for a while now, but no one listens. You'd be better off turning off that flashy decorative signage around the store's roof."

"It's a landmark in the darkness. We can't do that. The information from our headquarters said that the uninterruptible power supply has enough capacity to maintain this area until tomorrow morning."

"That's not true at all. I checked the UPS out the back. What your headquarters probably means is that if it's just for these decorative signage lights and the signboard streetlight that you're using as massive lanterns, then it might last twelve hours. But you continued to run the fridges and freezers inside the store on the UPS after the power went out last night, didn't you? Until the shelves were emptied? There's no way that much electricity is left. It's already late at night. The power will run out before the change of day."

"Oh, I see."

"Let me see the meter and the power consumption. I'll tell you exactly how many minutes we have left to draw from the supply. If it's a modern commercial UPS, and we can open the panel, it should display the number of hours or minutes remaining in operation at the current rate you're drawing power."

"Sorry, but I've never had to check anything like that myself. Could I ask that you handle everything relating to that kind of thing? But, I'd prefer it if we didn't turn off the decorative signage lights."

"Surely it will be fine to turn them off? This isn't a train station convenience store. We're in the middle of a residential area. Having just one giant lantern should suffice as a landmark. If you're looking to provide light for the crowd gathering around the store, there's a more efficient way to do it. Just remove a bulb or two from the store lights and hang them outside as makeshift lanterns…that should be enough. People can't go expecting anything fancy, like having light to read a book, during an emergency. And besides, you've got nothing to sell, so there's no need for bright light inside the store. A DIY lantern will work just fine. If you do it right, you'll be consuming a fifth of what you're consuming now."

"Thank you, if you could please take care of it?" Minami turned to the crowd once more. "Is there anyone else here who can help with this kind of work? Someone with experience in electrical work or from an electrical engineering faculty?"

"Oh, I can probably help. I'm an electrical maintainer for a railway company. I don't know what electrical systems you have set up here, but I'll be more helpful than the average man." A middle-aged man who had been waiting for the next delivery of items came forward.

In the end, around a dozen people offered their assistance. Among them was a young person who had a mere one week's experience working at a convenience store. She had apparently quit after a customer got angry at her for not remembering a brand of cigarettes, a situation all too common at convenience stores.

Following that, there were individuals who, while not possessing any special skills, had time on their hands and were willing to do cleaning or whatever else was needed. Young people who said they weren't even looking for a part-time wage also came forward.

Everyone followed the set procedures and quickly got to work. In the middle of it all, two delivery vehicles finally showed up. An escort from the company's motorcycle squad was leading them to assist with traffic control through intersections without working traffic lights.

Twenty cardboard boxes. The items inside them weren't exactly convenience store products, but more akin to disaster relief supplies. Every box contained pretty much the same things — sports drinks, dairy milk, biscuits, flashlights, batteries, formula milk, and women's sanitary products. An accompanying notice stated that it was all to be provided free of charge. For families, there were small quantities of instant ramen and ready-to-eat dry packed rice.

A portable gas stove and propane gas cylinders for boiling water were also provided. The next delivery would be in six hours. Even with these supplies, Minami realised they would barely manage to serve half the queue, so she once again borrowed the handheld megaphone and called out for help.

Although Minami was specialising in distribution economics and had thought she could do the necessary calculations, she figured that in this situation it might be faster to seek help from someone simply good at maths. Knowledge up to Maths III should suffice, she reckoned, although frustrated she couldn't do it herself.

This time, an elegantly dressed elderly man stepped forward. He was accompanied by a Yorkshire Terrier, as if he just happened to be out for a walk at this time.

"Would you happen to be a maths teacher, sir?"

"No, no, I'm not exactly a mathematician. I teach econometrics at one of the national universities. I was just walking by before supper. But my specialty is probably a bit much for what you're after…"

"No, not at all! It's exactly what we need, sir! Sorry, I mean… Professor…? I understand this might be a rather mundane task for someone of your expertise, but the supplies we've just received here are limited and the queue is long. For now, we need to give something to these people so they can be on their way. Could I ask for your help in finding the best solution for fair distribution?"

"That sounds like a pre-higher maths problem. No need for calculus or anything. A first-year middle school student could handle it."

"Maybe, but we could still use your help, sir. As a volunteer…"

"Hmm. Well, if that's the case, this should only take about five minutes. Get me some paper and a pencil. I need to know the number of people in line, along with the gender and age distribution. We might consider quantifying the reliability of their self-reported family compositions too, but since this is Setagaya, I expect people are reasonably honest. The distribution shouldn't be too large."

"I'll leave it all to you, sir. I'll get you a table and chair, and someone to assist you."

This is why you should never underestimate the residents of Setagaya City, Minami thought. Somehow, it looked like they could make it work. Minami Komachi vowed to do what she could to protect this light, as she recalled the faces of her family; faces she hadn't recalled for a long time until just recently.

———

Futoshi Tanaka thought there were a few too many boxes piled up at the side of the convenience store. The delivery vehicles had made this store their final stop in Hachioji City, unloaded the supplies, and then headed off towards Otsuki City. From here, he needed to transport the supplies to a store near the foot of Mt. Takao. Even with some young volunteers to carry them, twenty boxes might have been too many. Besides, the gathering crowd was now staring at him.

"We should open these and sell what's inside," he heard someone say. Tanaka needed to move the supplies quickly.

An approaching mass of students startled him. They approached in two lines, the beams from their flashlights stretching out in front like some form of illumination.

"We're on time, right?" Yusuke Shimoyama asked Tanaka.

"Err, I guess so…But what's with all these people?"

"Looks like around three-hundred."

"But there are children here, too?"

"The university was designated as a shelter, and it has a competition-standard gym. Word got out that the university would give students credits for volunteering in the local neighbourhood. Those students, plus parents and children who want to experience this event have come along. And just in case, six members from the hiking club are bringing up rope and stretchers."

"Oh, I see…" said Tanaka in disbelief. "Umm, can I entrust these supplies with you? It's three k's to the store at the edge of town."

"Should only take thirty minutes. We'll get members of the sports club to take it. Are you wearing business shoes, Mr. Tanaka?"

"Oh, no. They have running shoe soles. Besides, Trail One is paved all the way to the top. You've never climbed it at night?"

"Of course I have. We all used to dash up and run back down. The night view from up there is beautiful. But I don't think you can see Tokyo Tower."

"Understood. It will be fun when we arrive. Let's hope we can see it."

Shimoyama tasked the sports club members with the stacked supplies then set off.

This is reckless, thought Tanaka. Should something happen, his ethical responsibility as the leader would come into question and he would come under scrutiny by both the police and the company. He had assumed there would be about ten people at most.

As they walked along, Tanaka decided to select people to run safety management. He appointed individuals to forge ahead of the main column and ensure safety at the traffic intersections. For the rear guard, he designated members of his sales team.

The traffic congestion in this area had already eased. But with the traffic and street lights out, private vehicles were sometimes seen speeding through the intersections. And with everyone's phone batteries dead, getting lost would be a disaster. In the worst-case scenario, someone might realise they were lost only after having left the residential area into the mountains.

Tanaka instructed the students to ensure that the column didn't break formation and to pay attention to anyone who fell behind. Why on earth did the BCP headquarters chief send all that unnecessary information to the Hachioji area, a place where Tokyo Tower wasn't even visible? It was as if they were being ordered to climb Mt. Takao.

———

Minami Komachi set up one of the summer festival sales tables at the front of the convenience store to manage transactions. She did wonder why people would go out of their way to spend their money on supplies they could probably get for free at a community hall or primary school.

She imagined people huddled together in dimly lit spaces in primary schools that likely didn't have power generators. Just like insects and fish, humans also gravitate towards light. And perhaps, civilised people affirm their existence by spending money?

It also seemed that half the people here were lined up as if at a festival, enjoying the event of buying a box of biscuits, a bit like when elderly people form long queues at supermarkets to buy eggs on special. It wasn't about saving or spending money, but interacting with other humans.

From the inside of the store, young Yasu emerged holding the most recent fax. Finally, the mystery of Tokyo Tower was revealed.

"Today at 20:00, the lights of Tokyo Tower will be turned on. It will be illuminated for only fifteen minutes. If successful, it will be illuminated at this time every evening until power is restored. Please disseminate this information to local residents!" Once again it was signed off by the BCP headquarters chief.

"What even is this? Why the heck would they do something like this? And we can't even see Tokyo Tower from here anyway."

"I don't recall ever being able to see it. Actually, it's a bit of a walk from here, but there's a pedestrian bridge over Kanpachi-dori Avenue. If you go up there, I'm sure there's a spot where you can just see Tokyo Tower."

"The locals know that you can see Tokyo Tower from there, right? If people flood in to see it, it could cause a panic. It could even lead to a stampede. Wouldn't it be better to prevent it?"

"Should we speak to the police?"

"Good idea. We can't abide by something like this, even if HQ ordered it."

Minami showed the paper to the police officer outside the store, and sought a decision. The officer also expressed disapproval. "I think this is dangerous…" he said and made a radio call to the police station for advice.

But the order from the main station was completely unexpected. They were prepared for the situation. They would send additional officers, and he was instructed to lead the residents to a spot where Tokyo Tower could be seen and manage the crowd to prevent accidents.

Minami couldn't understand why the police were being made to expend effort just for the illumination of Tokyo Tower. But at least it would temporarily reduce the number of people here.

Standing on top of the beer bottle crate, Minami explained 'Tokyo Tower 20:00' to the crowd. Through the handheld megaphone she explained that while it couldn't be seen from here, there was a place where it could. And for those who really wanted to see it, the police officer here would lead the way, so please follow along. Like a herd of lemmings, the queue dispersed, and people began to move off in the direction of Kanpachi-dori Avenue.

"What's with these people…?"

"Let's go too," suggested young Yasu.

"Why? You can see Tokyo Tower anytime, can't you? Besides, what about the store?"

"There are other part-timers here, and the only thing left to steal is cash. We can just put that in the office for now. I think tonight's Tokyo Tower illumination will be something special, don't you?"

"I'm not really that keen, but I guess it wouldn't be a crime to take a break." Minami quickly moved the cash into the office. The proprietress was fast asleep, covered in cardboard and removed from the whole situation. Minami closed and locked the door quietly so as not to wake her.

They walked through the residential area. It was pitch black, lit only by the flashlights people carried.

"Yasu! Yasu! I can't see you!"

"Should we hold hands?"

"No, but I'll hold your elbow," said Minami as she grabbed Yasu's right elbow.

"Whoa, look up! This is a totally different Tokyo!" The night sky was full of twinkling stars. Probably twice…no, five or ten times more than normal.

"Wow, so this is a true starry night."

The engines of a helicopter or aeroplane could be heard overhead. Although it wasn't the middle of the night, it was still quite loud. Minami thought it spoiled the mood.

————

Prime Minister Aso left the conference room and returned to the Executive Office on the next floor up. The heated discussion had gone round in circles and failed to reach a conclusion. A small number of trusted advisors filled the room, dimly lit by the faint glow of LED lanterns.

"So, *Echigo-ya*, how is it turning out?" the prime minister asked, addressing Ito, the former colonel.

"I intend it to be perfect, but we're doing this without rehearsal. I'm praying it goes well."

Ito was holding a satellite phone to his ear, connected by a cable from outside. The windows of the Executive Office were designed to block electromagnetic waves, so satellite phones didn't work even when right next to them. Ito's phone had to be connected to an antenna on the roof. "...I told you not to fly, didn't I? Isn't air traffic control the jurisdiction of the Ministry of Transport? If you don't care about losing that authority, then I'm okay with sending a warning from an SDF plane! Please direct all helicopters from the Metropolitan Police, the Tokyo Fire Department, and TV stations to move out to sea. We issued this order twice since this afternoon, so why are they still flying? Please give the citizens of Tokyo a moment of peace... The imagery isn't the problem. We have drones equipped with 8K cameras at different altitudes — low, medium, and high...flying quietly."

"Give me that," said the prime minister, irritated, and snatched the satellite phone from Ito. "Listen up! Who do you think you are? This is the prime minister! If you can't follow orders, you'll be taking a one-way ASDF flight to Sado Island or the Rishiri-Rebun Islands first thing tomorrow morning! You have three minutes to get those choppers outta here or I'll personally launch SAMs at them, right from the top of this building! If the TV stations kick up a stink, tell them to capture the moment the PM fires off the first missile! They'd better hope those TV choppers are equipped with chaff and flares!"

Two minutes later, every helicopter had left the airspace above Tokyo and headed into Tokyo Bay. Prime Minister Aso went to stand by the window, but Tokyo Tower wasn't visible from the Prime Minister's Office. However, a fifty-inch screen flicked on, displaying footage from a drone overtop the Prime Minister's Office. It was dark; the only things discernable were patrol lights; over twenty sets of them flashing, including those on riot police vans.

"Time is dragging on, isn't it, Prime Minister..."

"What do you think about this whole situation?"

"One thing I'm glad about not being in uniform anymore is that, in times like this, I can say without any hesitation that I'm no longer in a position of responsibility."

"The Ground, Maritime and Air Chiefs, you see, it's written all over their faces — they think we have no choice but to support Taiwan and join the fight. But they wouldn't dare say it out loud. They seem determined to make it seem like my decision."

The drone zoomed out its camera and began to ascend. The entirety of the capital city of Tokyo, engulfed in darkness, was displayed on the monitor. The only lights were those of convenience store street lamps and the red lights of emergency vehicles. Tokyo Tower should have been within this view, but it was utterly unclear where it was. It could even have been right in the centre of the picture for all they knew.

"The countdown has begun!"

———

At 19:55 the group reached Takaosan Station where the terminus of the Takao Tozan Cable and Mt. Takao observatory were located. They were cutting it fine. The elevation here was four-hundred and seventy metres, although not the very summit of Mt. Takao. The view was clear, but of course, there was no cityscape to behold below. It was pitch dark in every direction.

Tanaka issued instructions through a megaphone. He allowed families with children to go ahead, but asked that they don't get too close to the fence. In the worst-case scenario, the danger was not falling, but being crushed to death.

With sixty seconds to go, he ordered all flashlights to be switched off, but he handed one to a student standing in the direction of Tokyo Tower, and told everyone to look that way.

With thirty seconds to go, everyone started counting down. Although Tanaka wasn't exactly sure what to expect, having climbed all this way, he hoped the plan would succeed.

"Ten, nine, eight…"

Everyone, Tanaka included, cast their gaze in the direction of Tokyo Tower.

"…three, two, one, zero!"

At that moment, a single pillar of fire appeared far into the distance.

"Hey! Is that Tokyo Tower? Is it, Dad?" asked a child.

The building was levitating on the horizon in the pitch darkness. It looked like a beam of light floating in the sky.

"So this is what Hamada wanted to show the people of Tokyo…"

It seemed unbelievable, a scene close to a miracle. It was worth the climb up here. Civilization amid despair; a manifestation of the will of the people of Tokyo, of the whole nation, to rise up from this darkness.

———

There was a gasp in the Prime Minister's Executive Office the moment Tokyo Tower lit up. It was as if the colossal Tokyo Tower, seen from above, was floating in space.

"Bravo, Echigo-ya!"

"Your praise deeply honours me, sir."

"How long have you been preparing for this?"

"Well, two years ago on a weeknight, all the Japan Rail lines were forced down because of a substation fire. But I noticed that people waiting for taxis or walking home were posting on social media how much the light of Tokyo Tower cheered them up. So we put together a plan with the authorities. The light here is 130 percent brighter than usual. And since there are no other lights in the vicinity, it should appear several times brighter to the human eye. Incidentally, similar plans were made for Yokohama Marine Tower, Tsutenkaku in Osaka, and Fukuoka Tower — landmarks in those cities."

"I probably shouldn't ask this, but did you scrape together dozens of power supply trucks for this?"

"It's not really just a matter of how many trucks we've used. These power trucks can power dialysis machines for hospitals or bring light to gyms where evacuees are staying. The opposition will have a go at us no doubt. They'll gripe about you ordering something this 'wasteful' at the next Diet session. How will you respond, sir? The brunt of the criticism will fall on you."

"In response I will stand tall and say it boldly, 'Do you remember where you were and what you were doing at that time? I was at the Prime Minister's Office, watching the moment Tokyo Tower regained its warm light. Tokyo Tower is a landmark to celebrate the rebirth of Japan from the ashes of war, a symbol of the post-war recovery, high economic growth, the bubble economy's collapse, and the long recession that followed for thirty years. At that moment, when Japan was once again facing hardship and the light of Tokyo Tower came back on, it was a scene so ordinary yet filled with awe and moved me as a Japanese person. Every night has its dawn. Tokyo Tower represented my vow to the nation that we would overcome this crisis…' That's how I'll respond."

"In Tokyo, probably five million people, and if you include the neighbouring prefectures, six million people must be witnessing this illumination. Tomorrow, the number will likely double," said Ito.

"Well, it's a great spectacle. Now, guess I'd better return to the endless tedium of meetings…"

Ito had a satisfied look on his face. It felt like he had completed a major task.

———

The stream of people heading for the pedestrian bridge in Setagaya hadn't moved an inch as the clock struck eight o'clock pm. They could hear cheers from afar, but it seemed unlikely they'd make it in time. It looked like it would take another twenty minutes for the crowd to clear. It felt like a Tamagawa Fireworks Festival day.

Yasu suddenly remembered something and grabbed Minami's hand. "There's a glass office building nearby!"

"But we can't go into an office building, can we?"

"It's fine! Come with me," he said, pulling Minami's hand firmly.

They ran through the residential neighbourhood. As soon as they reached Ring Road 8, Yasu looked in the opposite direction of Tokyo Tower and pointed, saying, "Look, over there!" There were no lights nearby. But Tokyo Tower was clearly visible on the glass-panelled building. Local residents who had realised they wouldn't make it onto the pedestrian bridge before the lights went out had also gathered to look up at the wall of the building on the opposite side, cheering at the sight. Couples took selfies on their smartphones.

"So that's Tokyo Tower!" Minami had never gone up Tokyo Tower, nor did she have any particular sentiment towards it. But tonight Tokyo Tower was undeniably special. It stood as a beacon, offering comfort and courage to the people. She realised she would remember this spectacle, this moment, and everything that happened today. In many ways, it was a moment that gave meaning to people's lives, a testament to the resilience and hope that defines human spirit.

4

Great Cause

As the splendid illumination of Tokyo Tower came to an end, Ito, who had watched until the final moments, noticed that Commissioner Naoto Hiiragi, advisor to the Kanto Regional Police Bureau's National Cyber Unit, was in the room. His body language suggested he had matters to discuss with Ito, rather than the prime minister.

"Very well done, Mr. Ito. I'm sure it will raise the spirits of many of our citizens."

"You don't look as though you've brought glad tidings."

"Well…" Hiiragi gestured Ito over to the side by the wall. "As a matter of fact, there were a few mishaps during last night's pursuits. It seems we lost track of some of the subversive operatives and radicalists after the sabotage acts. There were so many pursuits we even resorted to borrowing personal cars from office staff. These days, the operatives have got smarter, equipping their cars with rear dash cams, checking the footage later to see if they were followed or not…The group who blew up the undersea cable landing station in Chiba…"

"Don't tell me you let those guys slip?"

"Yes, my apologies. We thought we were tailing them perfectly until they returned to Tokyo. When it got lighter and we hit the morning traffic in the city centre, we had one of our cars drive by them the opposite way to get a look inside as they passed. But the driver was all alone in there. We have no idea where he dropped off the passengers. With the power outage, surveillance cameras are down everywhere, leaving us quite at a loss. We've also failed in several other pursuits. Though I believe we've managed to follow about 60 percent of them..."

"In other words, you let 40 percent of them slip? Did you get any photos you could use for facial identification?"

"No, sorry. The driver had on thick sunglasses and a mask. We deployed a drone too, but it was too high…"

"That's very clumsy."

"Yes. But there was one saving grace. There wasn't any evidence that they knew they were being pursued."

"Well, if a hacker gets detected before breaking in, you wouldn't call them a good hacker, would you? That's hardly consoling."

"Yes, well…we're collecting data from surveillance cameras prior to the blackout and investigating the origins of the vehicles. We'll find some sort of lead eventually, but as it stands, we're currently unable to stop them before their next acts. I need to report this to the prime minister…"

"You probably should. But adding to the prime minister's worries won't necessarily lead to a positive outcome…But you'll need to recover from this."

"Yes. I've already reported it to the Deputy Chief Cabinet Secretary…and copped a bit of a dressing down…"

"Probably because you're sending a dozen cars for every one of theirs and still losing them. Anyway, shit happens, I guess. You can make up for it by doing your job well."

"I'm truly sorry. By the way, I've been meaning to ask, and maybe I've been hearing it wrong, but what does *Echigo-ya* mean?"

"Ah, that, hah! I'll tell you the story when we get time. It's nothing too important. Something about laughing through even the most serious things."

Ito put on his favourite Panama hat, stepped into the hallway and made some calls on the satellite phone. Everyone had been flocking to use the same phone, so it had become hard to get hold of. He conveyed his gratitude to the executives and engineers of the electric power companies and others who had co-operated with the Tokyo Tower illumination plan. The photographs of it will be dressed up like pages from a sports paper. They'll have convenience stores print them out and display them in a manner reminiscent of broadsheets from the Tokugawa period.

Undoubtedly, by this time tomorrow there will be a surge of people around Kanto to places where Tokyo Tower could be viewed. To offer a glimmer of hope amidst adversity was a fundamental tactic of psychological warfare. If the enemy sought to inflict despair by severing lifelines, we'll respond by instilling in the people an enduring hope, thought Ito.

———

Leading a covert operations team composed of ethnic Chinese from Vietnam, PLA Army First Lieutenant Kong Xueli, under the alias Nguyen Thi Lan, had arrived in Japan just three days ago. She and her team arrived posing as technical intern trainees. It had been a hectic three days. On the night of their arrival, they toured to the base of Tokyo Tower by taxi. Then late the following night, they headed to the Chiba coast to blow up the undersea cable landing station there.

They were heading back towards Tokyo in a van belonging to a cooperative far-left extremist group, but were offloaded once they reached Funabashi. It was a thrilling experience. While mid-motion in their van, they all transferred to a container truck that pulled up closely alongside, jumping into the open door on its side. Adrenaline rushed through them, blowing away any and all drowsiness.

They had been told that these cooperative groups were just make-believe revolutionaries playing a cosy game with the Japanese police who wanted more budget, but now they doubted the veracity of that story.

A minor problem did arise after they disembarked from the container truck in Edogawa Ward. By then, traffic congestion was already heavy in the downtown areas, leaving the car they planned to drive the rest of the way somewhat useless. Of course, all the trains had already stopped as well. To reach their destination in Setagaya to the south, they ended up having to walk twenty-three kilometres from Edogawa Ward in the east.

An irony of the success of the broader sabotage operation was that it rendered the internet unusable. They couldn't access any information on their smartphones. GPS was still available, though, so they managed to reach their Setagaya base by relying on maps they had downloaded beforehand and using GPS to show their location. It wasn't anything too difficult. Physical endurance training was part and parcel in the military, and above all, everyone was safe and buoyed by the success of the operation.

What did surprise them was the large masses of office workers early in the morning who, despite the circumstances, were commuting to their workplaces on foot. Convenience stores were open too, selling sports drinks on tables set outside. And with the city's surveillance cameras out of operation, it was a relief to be able to walk around without the usual need for caution.

By the afternoon they reached the technical intern trainee rental apartment. There was no electricity. Showers were cold as no hot water was available, but there was an ample supply of food and a portable gas stove ready for them, ensuring they faced no real discomfort. And anticipating the potential cutoff of water supply, enough portable toilets to last a week had been prepared for them as well.

Decoding an encrypted broadcast from their homeland received via shortwave radio, the message was clear: "All covert operations units have achieved remarkable success causing a nationwide blackout across Japan. The operational headquarters commends the valiant efforts of all comrades! Proceed with your covert activities with renewed vigour!" In celebration of their operation's triumph, they prepared Vietnamese-style fried rice, toasted to their success, and then collapsed into a deep sleep in their allocated rooms.

It was completely dark when First Lieutenant Kong was woken by a visit from a fellow collaborator. The utter silence made it difficult for her to fully wake up. She could occasionally hear voices calling out through megaphones, but to her non-Japanese ears they sounded like lullabies. The visitor, Dinh Lei Feng, had lived in Japan for many years and held a permanent residency permit. She had come here alone on a scooter that evening.

It was past seven thirty pm. Kong ordered everyone to get changed quickly. Not a word was said about last night's, or rather, this morning's operation.

Kong, who had her own room, quickly checked her makeup and asked Dinh in Vietnamese, "How's everything with work going?" For them and others who had lived as ethnic minorities near the Vietnamese border, Vietnamese was their mother tongue. Mandarin served as a common language learned in school, but Vietnamese was more comfortable for them.

"Today's a day off for everyone, except for those involved in their usual undercover work. There's no way to contact the agency in Hanoi. You know, some staff cycled twenty kilometres into the office today, despite knowing there was no work. Made me laugh; they're just like Japanese people. We've lived here too long, and we've been overly influenced by this society's culture and character. I sent them home, and told them there was no need to come in until the electricity and internet were restored and the trains were running again. You did check the encrypted message from the homeland, right?"

"Yes. It boosted morale. Will this break Japan? I thought I knew Japan quite well from my studies, but if I'm honest, I don't understand its policies or diplomacy. What principles and rules does this government operate on?"

"You're wasting your time thinking about it. For the past thirty years, this country has practised a policy of non-confrontation from top to bottom."

"Well, will Japan give in to Beijing's intimidations?"

"Japan has pressure from the U.S. to deal with as well. Although even the U.S. is on edge from Beijing's intimidations. The Japanese prime minister is a cunning old fox; he keeps his cards close. Beijing is probably struggling to figure him out."

They prepared their flashlights and decided to go out in pairs. Without the daytime crowds, they didn't feel the gaze of the Japanese on them. It was rather a carefree outing. But given the darkness and not fully remembering the way, they were ordered in no uncertain terms not to get lost.

Nights were similar to this in both Hanoi and their hometown, so they walked without any sense of unease. The difference here, though, was the ability to roam around in this darkness without fear of assault — not something they could do in Hanoi.

There was a steady flow of people. Convenience stores were open, yet devoid of goods to sell. But people paused to examine notices displayed on the windows and entrances of these stores, and listened carefully to high school students relaying the messages on these notices through megaphones.

This is the strength of a homogeneous Asian society, thought Kong. Once something happens, people naturally come together and co-operate. In contrast, in the West, racial conflicts begin first, followed by class struggles, leading to societal divisions.

The flow of people was heading towards a park opposite the local train station. It was a fairly large park, but it didn't seem like there was anything in particular there. People were murmuring "Tokyo Tower…" among themselves, but it wasn't clear what they meant.

At the edge of the park, the faint lights of a convenience store could be seen. A patrol car was there, with its red lights flashing. The darkness wasn't total, but it wasn't light enough for the faces of people standing close by to be visible. Kong was worried and hoped no one would get lost. Just before eight o'clock, the red lights of the patrol car went out.

"Turn your flashlights off!" yelled someone, and everyone switched them off in an instant.

The moment Kong looked down to turn off her flashlight, a loud gasp rose from the crowd. She looked up and saw beyond a grove of trees the towering golden figure of Tokyo Tower shining brightly.

"Beautiful!" everyone murmured in unison. It glowed gold, as if clad in real gold.

Despite the distance, Kong thought it was far more beautiful than the night view they had seen on their first day. "It's incredible," she said in wonder.

"I've been looking at that old tower for many years," said Dinh, "but tonight's radiance is something special. The surrounding darkness makes it look several times more beautiful than usual. Incredible, isn't it? But it shouldn't be possible with just its own power generators."

"Why are they even doing this?"

"Probably to raise the spirits of the citizens who have been down because of the blackout. Really, this regime, or this administration rather, is pretty formidable."

She lowered her voice and whispered to Kong. "It's also a declaration of war against us. It signifies, 'If you initiate this, as a nation, as a people, Japan will rise to meet your challenge.'"

In the midst of that awe-inspiring moment, Kong felt a chill run down her spine. Although Japan had fallen into hard times, she had once risen as the conqueror of Asia and had challenged American dominance twice: once through war and the second time through economic power. She cautioned herself not to underestimate such a formidable opponent.

———

Domon also saw it from Camp Naha in Okinawa. It wasn't a live broadcast, but the footage from a drone sent by the Ministry of Internal Affairs and Communications was received by NHK's Naha station via satellite and then broadcast throughout Okinawa and to the world. The footage was accompanied by a statement from the prime minister: "We have been backed into a difficult situation, but we will never surrender. We will maintain the independence of our nation, apprehend the perpetrators of terrorist acts, and retaliate against the country that sent them."

While watching the television at his command post, Domon murmured, "Tokyo Tower sure is beautiful when you see it like this. Makes you sit up straight and take notice."

According to NHK, a simultaneous lighting event had taken place across municipalities nationwide, each featuring their landmark towers. Classic Ito, thought Domon.

"Is this really okay? To announce retaliation against China like that?" Machida asked in puzzlement.

"China knows full well that it's all just talk; not that they'd brag that they were the ones behind it, anyway."

"Could this be a case of shock doctrine, you know, using a crisis to slip through an agenda? Maybe the power and internet haven't even really gone down?"

"I really doubt even Ito would go that far. There have been actual explosions around the country. But supposing shock doctrine is at play here, the purpose wouldn't be to stir up hatred among the populace and drive them to war. Our prime minister might be good with money, but he's not interested in that kind of stuff. If anything, it would be to make the people aware of the gravity of the situation. But this light, though… this will kindle hope."

They could hear footsteps in the hallway. They weren't quick footsteps; if anything they sounded rather heavy. Colonel Go Hakuba, Commanding Officer of the Amphibious Rapid Deployment Brigade's 1st Amphibious Rapid Deployment Regiment, appeared and bowed rigidly. He was in combat uniform, but he looked refreshed and cleanly shaven. "Sir, do you mind if I have a word with you?"

"Of course." With a glance, Domon ordered his subordinates out of the room, then stood to receive Hakuba.

"Care for a tea or coffee? Or I can fetch something for you to eat…"

"No need for that, sir."

"Fine…" Domon sat back down. "Please have a seat."

"If I may please stand in place, sir. I have come to apologise."

"I'm not the actual Amphibious Brigade Commander. That is unnecessary."

After Hakuba landed with his unit on Uotsuri Island, he tried to lead a small number of troops in a *banzai* charge against enemy forces. He was stopped just in time by one of Domon's men, then was sent back under disciplinary action on a charge of command disarray.

"Are you alright now?"

"Yes, sir. I was sent back to Camp Miyakonojo, where I underwent questioning by the security unit there and received two days of intensive counselling. But in the end I wasn't censured."

"That's a relief. Given that we are in wartime, there's no room for dishing out punishments and such. Having the Amphibious Brigade Commander taken prisoner and a regimental commander compromised will affect the cohesion of the unit. If you're feeling responsible for what transpired there, you shouldn't. You weren't even on the island when the troops lost their lives. The fault lies solely with my misjudgment."

"It was my regiment, and they were my troops. I can all but take responsibility for the results. I heard you had submitted a formal recommendation for my return?"

"Hardly. I'm not part of the Defense Academy clique, and don't have that kind of influence. All I did was mention that you seem well-regarded by your colleagues and subordinates, so this incident might be overlooked."

"Thank you, sir." Hakuba bowed deeply.

"Considering what's to come, we can't afford to lose our composure every time there's a casualty. We both need to redeem ourselves. I can simply submit my resignation, but you, you're the star of your cohort. You have a duty to live up to that. I was never one to be on the first track to promotion like you...By the way, where is the regiment's command HQ located again?"

"We're borrowing a room from the U.S. Navy up at White Beach on the eastern side of the island. I'm heading back there after this."

"Alright. It's a heavy burden. We don't know when the PLA's assault on Taiwan will begin. It could be tomorrow, a week, or even a month from now. Our government will undoubtedly agonise over it, but ultimately, some form of military support will likely be provided. What are we doing about the garrison on Uotsuri Island?"

"We're making arrangements for a mainland unit to take over should we be mobilised for Taiwan…assuming we have air and sea superiority."

"Indeed, we can forget supporting Taiwan without that."

"Is there any plan for the release of the Brigade Commander and others?"

"Apparently there was quite a dispute over it. The Chinese side wants to repatriate them as soon as possible as a way of destabilising the SDF. The Japanese side has been refusing, citing the blackout as the reason, but it seems they're returning to Niigata Airport first thing tomorrow morning. Given the situation, they'll likely be in the custody of the Public Security Bureau for some time. It looks like the Brigade Commander will be taking responsibility in the form of his resignation. That speech was…unfortunate." Domon frowned. When the captured Amphibious Rapid Deployment Brigade officers were transported to China on the air-cushioned landing craft, they read statements prepared by the Chinese side in front of cameras. Although their position might have left them no choice, the prime minister was furious, and there was widespread condemnation within the GSDF officer ranks. "On the matter of support for Taiwan, I've heard that the Joint Staff Office is currently drawing up maps. The Amphibious Brigade has been secretly studying potential landing sites for years in preparation for supporting Taiwan, so we should align our thoughts when there's time. That's the situation as it stands."

"Understood."

"And if you keep dwelling on that matter from before, consider it a debt owed. A debt incurred on the battlefield can be repaid on the battlefield. But towards your subordinates, you need to continually prove through your judgement and command abilities that you've recovered. But you won't be able to achieve this overnight."

"Yes, sir. I understand."

Major General Domon stood, bowed to Colonel Hakuba, and ordered him to return to his unit. A leader who has spent years in the trenches with his troops might easily be forgiven for a blunder. But those thrusters like Hakuba who are frequently changing roles and climbing the promotion ladder have little time to assert control over their troops and must prove that they possess the appropriate abilities for the road to success. This would be something difficult for others to understand, Domon thought.

———

No one knew how many hours the meeting on the fourth floor of the Prime Minister's Office had lasted. Although some people switched out, and the prime minister occasionally stepped out for restroom breaks, the three SDF chiefs of staff had not left the room at all, nor had there been any breaks for meals.

Junior officials and uniformed personnel were constantly coming and going with their notes, but the conversation went in circles. Just when it seemed like progress was being made, they inevitably ended up at the same deadlock. A difficult labour within a difficult labour, once five hours had passed, everyone had acknowledged that no conclusion would be reached. The meeting had transformed into one solely for identifying problems.

Hiroshi Kuwabara, Parliamentary Vice-Minister of Defense, stood his ground, and continually advocated for Taiwan's defence, at times even shouting at the top uniformed officers in front of the prime minister.

The table was a mess. Empty coffee cups had been left on it, and the coffee pot placed on the table would quickly empty every time it was refilled. The fact that water had to be boiled on a cassette stove in the Prime Minister's Office made the whole scene all the more pitiful.

Two battery-operated air purifiers were brought in for Prime Minister Aso who couldn't part with his cigars. He stood in front of the monitor with a lit Cuban cigar, spreading its strong smell throughout the room, while listening to a brief by GSDF Chief of Staff General Yasuo Ushijima. The room was still only being lit by lantern light, so the monitor cast a dazzling glow. It was like being at a movie theatre.

"This is being recorded in the minutes, right?" Prime Minister Aso asked Soichiro Katakura, Senior Deputy Minister for Foreign Affairs.

"Yes, that's correct. I believe that falls under the jurisdiction of the Cabinet Office. It will be transcribed and likely made public in about a quarter-century. If the Ministry of Foreign Affairs were to intervene, it could remain classified as a state secret for even longer, perhaps half a century."

"Make sure to note down that I was puffing on cigars here. Future generations should know that a policy determining the fate of Japan was decided through a painfully long meeting."

"Yes, sir. I agree."

"So, what's the scenario?" pressing the Chief of the GSDF to continue.

"This is, strictly speaking, one hypothetical scenario for the defence of Taiwan. However, it's also a prediction that has a high likelihood of happening, around sixty to seventy percent certainty."

In front of Aso, across the oblong table, was a fifty-inch screen displaying a map of Taiwan which allowed them to zoom in and out. Zooming out, the map extended west to India and north to the Aleutian Islands. When zooming in, it detailed every single landmark on an urban map of Taipei.

"No matter how huge the PLA may be, or even if they mobilise civilian ferries, there's a limit to the size of the initial force they can land. Even if they destroy all of Taiwan's air bases with ballistic and cruise missiles, they'll only be able to initially land and sustain a force of about one-hundred thousand. In response, the Taiwanese military would confront them with a hundred thousand regular army troops and twice that number in reserve. In fact, the strategy for such a war has always been somewhat consistent across the ages. The initial goal will be to advance on the capital and demand the opposing government's surrender, and ask them if it is acceptable to turn the capital into rubble. Then, if a puppet government can be installed, the war would end — without the involvement of Japan or the U.S."

"I think I'd prefer that. It means no one has to die. We don't have to bomb the semiconductor factories. By next week, Taiwan will be operating as if nothing happened, right?"

Kuwabara alone shook his head in disagreement. "But if the Taiwanese government doesn't yield to any threats, the PLA will advance towards Taipei. They won't need tanks. In modern warfare, tanks can easily be destroyed by drones or missiles. Brutal urban warfare would ensue. One key factor, or element, is how long this urban combat drags on. Whether Taipei falls in three days, holds out for a week, or, like Beirut or other Middle Eastern cities, becomes a pile of rubble but endures for more than a month...It's impossible to predict.

"Taiwan, like Japan, is mountainous, and being drawn into mountain warfare would be extremely disadvantageous for the PLA. Conversely, the Taiwanese military might count on our military support and commit to delay tactics, aiming to lure the PLA into mountainous regions. Even with fewer troops, they could still inflict significant casualties on the enemy.

"While the enemy is fighting to take control of Taipei, Taiwan would likely work on maintaining their front lines and engage in diplomatic efforts to seek military support from the rest of the world, in particular direct intervention from Japan and the United States. The Taiwanese military would avoid pointless assaults, and instead focus on endurance and buying time. Conversely, knowing that time is at risk, the PLA would be determined to bring about a swift conclusion to the conflict."

"So what's the problem for you guys?"

"Well, suppose we continue to sit silently and observe the unfolding situation, and the PLA starts its campaign on Taipei without attacking Okinawa, leaving our forces intact and preserved. Then later, driven by international and domestic public opinion, we decide to join the conflict. Would we be able to conduct a successful landing operation then? Or, would speaking out against China's aggression from the start, getting involved right from the onset of hostilities, accepting ballistic missile attacks on Okinawa, and involving ourselves with the inevitable sacrifices lead to less depletion of our forces and contribute more effectively to Taiwan's defence? That's the question."

"So what's the answer?"

"It's hard to say. It depends on the damage taken at the onset of hostilities. If the PLA attacks us, it naturally means that part of the forces they would otherwise dedicate to conquering Taiwan would be diverted here, thereby lessening the pressure on Taiwan. It's possible that Taipei could repel the PLA with little to no damage. Whether the U.S. military participates in the fight directly or not, we would still fight with the full backing of the U.S. On the other hand, if we decide to wait and see how the situation unfolds, only engaging after feeling confident in Taiwan's ability to hold out, we might end up making the mistake of gradually committing our forces, which could be disastrous."

"Even if the U.S. military backs us up, soldiers will die, right? Japanese people."

"Prime Minister, in the defence of Uotsuri Island we would not have got off with such minimal casualties without American support. The forces that landed on the island would have been annihilated in no time, and the escort fleet likely would have suffered a devastating blow. And the PLA would probably have already landed in Taiwan by now."

"Fine. I've asked a dozen times now, is this a *perilous situation around Japan*?"

"Before that, remember we already have a defence mobilisation order in effect for Uotsuri Island…"

"But we did recapture it, didn't we? So, the war should end there, right? We can't keep going on and on until the enemy's regime is overthrown, like in the old days. It doesn't look like the Chinese Communist Party is going to collapse anytime soon.

Mr. Stratton, do you, or the White House, think that Japan can deploy forces under the *Act for Perilous Situations in Areas Surrounding Japan*?"

Joe Stratton, Counsellor for Government Affairs at the U.S. Embassy, who was seated in a chair by the window, stopped taking notes and looked at the prime minister. "The White House fully understands that Japan is significantly constrained by her constitution. Regarding the Act in question, we understand that its interpretation can be very challenging. As an aside, we commend the performance demonstrated by the Self-Defense Forces over these past two weeks. After all, they managed to hold off China's invasion of Taiwan for two weeks. This is an astounding result and a significant military victory."

"The SDF did a good job as cannon fodder, didn't they? That's something worth praising, right? But let's put aside the niceties. From my perspective, it seems like the Empire is making Japan do the dirty work while firmly shaking hands with China behind the scenes. We've risked losing trade with China by getting involved in the Taiwan issue, yet it looks like the Empire is still indecisive and wavering, doesn't it?"

"It's as you say, sir. The strategic ambiguity we have maintained on Taiwan, much like the strategic patience Japan has continued to uphold, is clearly showing its limits. Neither strategy was formulated with the current level of China's monstrous escalation in mind."

"China took advantage of our indecisiveness. Katakura, what were the economic security risk factors again?"

"Yes, sir. As much as twenty percent of our trade is with China. It's been almost twenty years since China surpassed the United States in this regard. When China recently implemented planned domestic power outages as part of its own environmental policy, it affected all kinds of supply chains, from the raw materials for model kits to automobiles. The semiconductor shortage was widely reported as if it was the sole reason for the vehicle production slowdown, but the reality was that disruptions in parts procurement from China was also to blame. If Japan commits any deeper to the situation surrounding Taiwan, it will accelerate the slowdown of the entire Japanese economy.

"And it's not just about the economic impact in terms of numbers; unavoidable effects on the daily lives of citizens, similar to the mask shortages during the coronavirus pandemic, will also occur. For instance, the semiconductor shortage led to situations like people having to wait six months just for water heater repairs. There were shortages of parts for bicycles and motorcycles, and new houses were left without toilets to install...We'll end up being on the receiving end of these kinds of situations, meted out with clear intent to harass us. Whether it's worth accepting these trade disadvantages to help Taiwan, with its population of only twenty million, is the question. It's not just about money. After shedding the blood of our SDF personnel to protect it, what we'll get in return is an economic slowdown and actual disadvantages in daily life."

"Well, hardly seems worth it, does it?" said Aso, turning to look at Kuwabara. "Mr. Kuwabara, you've gone quiet. You tired?"

Kuwabara did in fact look exhausted, but he abruptly opened his mouth to speak. "Well, if trade and daily conveniences are so important, then maybe we should just become a vassal state to China. Or even better, one of its provinces, call ourselves the People's Republic of China Japan Province, and wave the red flag. Teach Mandarin instead of English. Hey, if that makes the citizens richer. Toilet bowls, bicycle tires, if needed, we should just make them domestically. If we switch to domestic products from the things we're currently buying from China for a pittance, wouldn't prices and wages go up?

"Regarding Taiwan, the Ministry of Foreign Affairs keeps making scary arguments about the population of a mere twenty million versus the huge market of 1.4 billion. But is that population of twenty million really so small that we can just forget about it? In Japan, where the population is shrinking, we can't ignore the loss of a highly purchasing-powerful and pro-Japanese market of twenty million. To put it bluntly, of that massive market of 1.4 billion, probably 70 percent are from households too poor to even own a car."

"Hmm…I see your point."

"Prime Minister, right as we speak, an enormous volume of military support supplies is arriving from the mainland United States."

The GSDF Chief requested to speak again. "It's not just by air; the transport fleet that set sail from the West Coast is already arriving in Japan. Two weeks was enough time to cross the Pacific and secure supplies. There're so many supplies arriving by air — missiles, artillery shells — that we're running out of places to store them."

"That's not free, is it? The bill for that proxy war will arrive eventually. And it'll be written at their asking price, no less."

"Continuing to be a part of the free world is a fundamental principle for our nation's prosperity."

"All that democracy and free economy stuff has faded quite a bit, hasn't it? Right, Mr. Stratton?"

"Yes, as you say, sir. On that point, all of us conscientious Americans deeply feel the responsibility. Unfortunately, America will probably become even more divided."

"It's surprising, isn't it? We believed that the democratic system was an absolute good and were happy to pay the cost for it. Yet, a psychopath who could turn everything upside down became your president and stirred up your country. I wish there was some reflection on how much trouble it caused to your allies. The fact that his influence has only grown stronger after leaving office suggests that American democracy isn't functioning properly, doesn't it?"

"Yes, I certainly have no rebuttal to that, sir." Even under the dim light of a lantern, the expression on Counsellor Stratton's face was one filled with mortification.

"By the way, has the Japan-Taiwan Parliamentary Friendship Association been able to contact the Taiwanese Presidential Office?"

"Yes, we've been able to communicate with their Ministry of Foreign Affairs via satellite phone."

"And they're saying they'll fight to the end?"

"Of course! The Office of the President calls me up to twenty times a day seeking a meeting with you, Prime Minister. They're pushing me hard, wondering why I'm having so much trouble organising a call with you. They've watched the crackdown in Hong Kong and chaos on the mainland that rivals even the Cultural Revolution. Anyone, no matter how carefree, would be convinced that this regime is absolutely no good. Isn't that obvious?"

"Even so, isn't Taiwan tied even more deeply to the Chinese economy than us? Can they really afford to oppose Beijing? They were all in a frenzy over just a single pineapple export ban."

"They'll manage. Isn't that precisely why we're striving to build a free market zone?"

"Do the Taiwanese people really think that? They're making a killing off the mainland economy. Incidentally, we may need to hurry up and reach a conclusion here."

"From a diplomatic strategic point of view, if Japan and the U.S. were to announce a full military commitment early on, it's not impossible that China might reconsider its invasion of Taiwan," said Katakura.

"China is threatening because they know full well that the Empire has no intention of full military involvement. If the 7th Fleet's aircraft carriers were deployed off the coast of Taiwan, this war would be over before it even started, don't you think?"

"It's complicated. Beijing is realising that their only chance to reclaim Taiwan is now, which is why they're in a hurry and feeling pressed. This is a game of chicken. The first side to flinch loses. If Beijing were to give up its ambitions because of Japan and the U.S. entering the fray, that would greatly damage the trust in their leadership and potentially lead to political upheaval. Knowing that, they might still initiate a war to leave a mark in history as having bravely taken up the challenge, even if they expect a crushing defeat."

"So, even if all the runways and airports south of the Amami Islands are destroyed, could the SDF still manage to defend our own territory and then provide support to Taiwan?"

"Absolutely! We can intercept ballistic missiles, and even if cluster bomb attacks from attack aircraft temporarily render the airfields and runways in the Ryukyu Islands inoperable, we've prepared a system to repair them quickly with the help of local construction firms. Also, our units are ready to evacuate to different locations, and we're confident they'll avoid annihilation. During the two weeks we held out on the Senkakus, we were able to prepare more than adequately." The GSDF Chief spoke, seeking nods of agreement from his Air and Maritime counterparts.

"I see. I'll take your word for it. I find it hard to believe that it was only the SDF that could prepare themselves quickly; the Prime Minister's Office's crisis management function was in a hell of a state. But I suppose that's what the military is for.

"But consider this — if China ignores Japan, but launches missiles at Taiwanese air bases, Taiwanese fighters will take refuge in Japan, say on Miyako or Ishigaki Islands. We're not going to shoot them down for violating our airspace, are we now? So if that happens, it would effectively mean Japan is supporting Taiwan's military. It would give China a reason to attack airfields in Okinawa. Now, I'm not saying I'm granting permission for Taiwanese jets to be warmly received. Don't get me wrong. We must think about our stance and response when we get dragged into this beyond our own free will. Beijing might, for example, preemptively warn that accepting Taiwan's fighters would be viewed as Japan participating in the war. On our part, we might have to declare that just because such a situation occurred, it doesn't mean we intend to join the fighting. Make sense? Let's call it a day here. Our *shoguns* here need to head back to Ichigaya, and the Ministry of Foreign Affairs has to go soothe both the China School and the North America faction.

"Mr. Stratton, please relay this to the White House: The Japanese have debated frankly for half a day, but no conclusion was reached. However, emphasise that this does not mean we are incapacitated as a concerned party. We have a precise grasp of the situation. And furthermore…" Aso paused to match the pace at which Joe Stratton was taking notes. "And furthermore," he continued, "we're not necessarily doubting the Empire's role as the *ketsu mochi*. You know what that means? The backer or protector…Anyway, Japan will act independently in defence of Taiwan if it aligns with our national interests. However, as it stands, we also want to watch Beijing's moves. We're deeply grateful for the material and moral support from the U.S. And feel free to add that I'm a crafty old fox."

"Understood, sir. I shall pass it on."

"Prime Minister, may I add something?" asked Kuwabara. "If a public opinion poll were conducted in Taiwan, invariably about 60 percent of the population would believe that the SDF will come to their rescue if there's an emergency. By taking action, we can also boost the morale of the Taiwanese people. We can buy time. And if Taiwan holds its ground, American public opinion is sure to shift."

"I don't agree, but well, hope is important, I guess. Both for the Japanese and the Taiwanese." With that, Prime Minister Aso stood up, and everyone in the room rose to see him out.

As he was leaving, he placed a hand on Kuwabara's shoulder as the latter attempted to stand. "Kuwabara, you really never stop worrying. Haven't you already honoured your obligation towards the National Defense Division and the Friendship Association?"

"It's for the sake of principle, Prime Minister. For a great cause. After all, a nation must have a great cause if it's to go to war, mustn't it? If that's forsaken, the nation will degenerate. I believe post-war Japan has lacked such a cause for a long time. After the country was rebuilt, there was no great cause for steering the nation's course. That's why no one could show resolve, and we remain unable to escape from this prolonged slump."

"Indeed, Mr. Kuwabara."

"Yes. The ancestor of yours who rose up against the Tokugawa shogunate, despite the slim chances of victory, would surely agree."

"I'll give it some thought."

The prime minister left the conference room with a contented expression. Kuwabara had no idea whether he had made an impact or not. He believed he had expressed 120 percent of what he intended to say, but whether or not it had reached the prime minister remained unclear.

———

Colonel Hikaru Shiba, a Mandarin Chinese teacher and martial arts instructor for the GSDF's Amphibious Rapid Deployment Brigade, was at a familiar hotel along the Tamsui River in Taipei. She had the misfortune of being in Taipei when the PLA's operation to capture Pratas Island began, which led to her being confined there. Consequently, she found herself in a position akin to a military attaché, involved in discussions with Taiwan.

Shiba was eating dim sums in the bar of the hotel's ground-floor lobby, brought by Lai Xiaochao, who had once stayed at her family home in Yokohama. Shiba was visiting Taipei to help Lai with the opening and running of a dim sum restaurant that had been left to her.

Like Japan, Taiwan was experiencing a blackout. The hotel had its own generator, but to conserve fuel, there were specific times when they would use it. Candles had been placed at several spots on the floor. It didn't make for a bad atmosphere, but the darkness was depressing. Although the hotel was located right behind one of Taipei's most bustling districts, not a sound from the city's hustle and bustle could be heard.

A young man named Wang Wenxiong, whom Shiba affectionately called Fumio, was also there with them. He was a graduate of Kyoto University's Faculty of Law, a member of the Taiwan-Japan Goodwill Association, the Deputy Director of the Kuomintang's Foreign Publicity Department, and, of course, he had a hidden side as well. The conversation among the three, under the candlelight, was a mix of Mandarin and Japanese.

"This is definitely seasoned for the Japanese palate," Shiba remarked.

"You think so? This place is for tourists, so that's a good thing. What do you think, Wang?"

"My palate has turned Japanese. I don't really get Taiwanese flavours anymore."

"Is there still gas left?" Shiba asked Lai, whom she looked upon as a daughter.

"Yes. On your advice, I stocked up on enough portable stoves and gas cylinders for each table. I gave about 70 percent to the local evacuation shelters. I've secured enough supplies, including rice, for us to hole up for a while. All the meat in the fridge has gone bad. Next time, we might have to buy our own power generator."

"You should probably evacuate the city soon, don't you think?"

"Are you joking? I'm Taiwanese too. I'll stay here and fight."

"I know it hasn't been long, and I'm confident I've taught you everything about running a restaurant, but I haven't taught you self-defence. I have no choice but to stay here… until we know whether we win or lose, but I can't afford to worry about you."

"I'll get someone to teach me how to shoot a gun."

"Wang, do you know somewhere where we can evacuate her to?"

"If we want somewhere nearby, there's my uncle's holiday house near Mt. Dongyan. We can still reach it on foot if the roads are blocked. But if we want somewhere further south…"

"Did you two even hear me?" protested Lai.

"You don't understand what war is. I didn't bring you back here just to show you people killing each other. You have to survive. Otherwise, I'll push you onto a relief flight back to Japan as a Japanese citizen."

"But planes aren't flying anymore! Radios aren't working either."

"What do you know, Fumio?"

"It looks like there are a few evacuation flights to Guam out of Hualien Airport on the east side of the island. They have to fly visually, so flying into Taipei is too risky. Japanese citizens looking to escape Taipei have been instructed to make their way to Hualien. But once it's on, no doubt missiles will rain down on there too."

"Fumio, can you please prepare a car so we can evacuate her."

"What about you, Miss Shiba? Are you going to stay?"

"There needs to be someone here to welcome our friends when they land. It'd be out of order if I left just as they were heading here."

"Do you think they'll join the fight?"

"General Domon's forces are on standby in Naha; he seems to think they will. But it's not really in our nature to put up our dukes over a mere blackout."

On the table was a colour printout of a terrestrial broadcast from Yonaguni Island received in Yilan County. It was the illumination of Tokyo Tower.

Shiba worried that many Taiwanese might mistake this as a declaration of the SDF's willingness to participate. Across Taiwan not a single radio signal could be picked up due to strong jamming from the mainland. But the news that lights were turned on at Tokyo Tower amidst the blackout across Japan spread from person to person like ripples over water.

Although not two hours had passed since that event, it was already lighting a beacon of hope in the hearts of the Taiwanese people. A beacon of hope that the Self-Defense Forces would come to their aid.

5

Evacuation

In Beijing, members of the elite PLA Joint Staff Department Operations Bureau gathered in a secluded corner in the Ministry of National Defense's Bayi Building. The room, rarely ever used, smelt mouldy and the lighting was dim. But it was essential that it hadn't been used recently. MERS infections, which had spread from the procurement office, were steadily consuming the Bayi Building. The virus made no distinctions between the office ladies of the procurement office and high-ranking admirals, attacking mercilessly and felling one healthy person after another.

Every possible measure was being taken to ensure the epidemic did not hinder the execution of operations. Major General Sun Yougang of the Operations Bureau, who was chairing the meeting, donned a medical mask and blue medical gloves.

This meeting was originally scheduled to be held in the Zhongnanhai state leadership compound, but officials wanted to avoid introducing the epidemic there. From Zhongnanhai, Pan Hongda, Deputy Director of the General Office of the Central Committee, was in attendance. He was a top elite, potentially a future party chairman. Everyone in the room wore grave expressions.

The guard was dressed in full protective gear, complete with dust covers for his shoes, and a mask and goggles for his face, such was the need for precaution. While a lockdown had been enforced across all of China, Beijing was still pushing on towards its long-held dream of reclaiming Taiwan.

"First off," began Major General Sun, "I'd like to commend the bureaus involved in the Taiwan and Japan blackouts. The Japan Operations Unit has achieved its difficult mission well. The Central Military Commission is also singing their praises. I heard the unit director got infected, but I don't know their name. The deputy should be in attendance here?"

A female officer seated at the end of the table caught Major General Sun's eye and said, "Sir, I'm Lieutenant Colonel Lin Hong, the third in command of the Japan Operations Unit. The deputy director was scheduled to attend, but developed a fever just earlier…"

"Oh! I hope you're alright, though?"

"Yes. I work directly across from the deputy director's desk, but as of now, I don't have a fever."

Everyone in the room visibly winced.

"In these circumstances…" Sun was at a loss for words.

"I've taken a PCR test every six hours, and I took a precautionary test before coming here as well."

"Keep that mask on. At any rate, well done. This should thwart Japan's intentions to join the conflict."

"What do you mean?"

"It means what it means. But am I detecting a difference of opinion in the unit…?"

"The cyber-attacks on Japan's infrastructure were not our idea. They were purely the idea of the Cyber Warfare Unit. Somehow, this has taken on a life of its own, as if it were a strategy of the Japan Operations Unit. We're somewhat perplexed by this."

"Huh? What's that supposed to mean now?"

"Sir, what I mean is, the Cyber Warfare Unit, as usual, boasted that Japan's network defences were as thin as a sheet and insisted that they be allowed to launch an attack. Before we could even consider it, the Central Military Commission approved it, so we were forced to mobilise our teams, including ones still in training, to infiltrate Japan and carry out simultaneous kinetic attacks. Sure, it was an operational success, but we haven't made any assessment of the effect this would have on the Japanese people."

"But it was a success…?"

"That depends on how you measure 'success'. Success in causing the blackout? Or the fact that the internet is unusable? The strategic objective was to demoralise the Japanese population and crush their will to resist. We haven't yet assessed the success of that."

"Well, let's have it now. Was it a success?"

"We see the blackout as being almost neutral in terms of our strategic objectives. So, no, we don't expect it to have an effect. Japanese people are accustomed to disasters. Every year, from summer to autumn, typhoons hit, causing floods and sometimes blackouts. Almost every decade, an unimaginably large earthquake occurs somewhere in the archipelago. Japan is a disaster-prone country. Panic is not going to break out over a blackout or the unavailability of the internet. All that will happen is a bit of inconvenience to daily life. Also, Japanese society is extremely homogeneous; complete strangers will unite and co-operate when the need arises. Even after this calamity ends, if it's reported on TV that China was behind it, they won't openly display hostility, nor will they necessarily cower before China. There were reports every day in Japan that their infrastructure was extremely vulnerable to cyber-attacks, so it was almost to be expected."

"So the whole thing was pointless?"

"Yes. Although, demonstrating our ability to blow up a substation in the very heart of Tokyo without hurting civilians was quite the performance."

"That wasn't the plan though, was it? The plan was to crush Japan's will to fight, but…"

"I did submit my concerns about all this in a memo, but it stopped at my supervisor. We've been so diligent in disinfecting even scraps of paper the last few days that it's probably lost now."

"To describe it as a 'performance', though…" Such disgraceful talk in the presence of an elite official from the General Office… Sun lamented inwardly that it was the end for her.

Pan, the General Office official, his face expressionless, raised his right hand, seeking to speak. "I am impressed by the frankness of your opinion. Indeed, this is exactly the reason I risked coming here; to hear views like these from the operations room. But what I want to ask the lieutenant colonel is, will Japan enter the war?"

"Yes, sir, eventually they will. It's just a question of whether it happens sooner or later. All we can do is try to delay Japan's entry into the conflict, even for a day or half a day. The U.S. military is providing an enormous number of supplies to them. It's unlikely that Japan will just sit by and watch Taiwan fall without putting them to use."

"The Rocket Force is awaiting orders. Infantry and tanks are starting to board ferries at the ports. We don't have much time. Do you think there is reason to hesitate on the operation?"

"No, sir. The idea of giving up on reclaiming Taiwan because we fear Japan's involvement is absurd in itself. But we should be prepared that Japan's entry into the conflict will pose obstacles to our mission in every conceivable way. We couldn't even seize Diaoyu Island, that small, uninhabited island…And while we were fixated on it, we lost three hundred of our latest fighter jets. As for our warships and their crew, more than a thousand have already been killed in action."

Pan Hongda found her interesting and watched her intently, but behind his goggles and mask it would have been difficult for the others to notice his focus.

"General Sun, I want to hear your opinion too. Are these sacrifices within our expectations? Or are we falling into the Concorde fallacy, given that we haven't laid a finger on Taiwan's main island yet?"

The *Concorde fallacy* was an ironic business term, also known as *sunk cost*, that referred to the phenomenon where, despite knowing that continuing development and investment would only result in massive losses, reluctance to waste resources already invested leads to persisting in the wasteful development. Last century, the Concorde was developed as a dream of supersonic passenger flight, but ended with just sixteen aircraft produced. Ultimately, an unfortunate crash forced the retirement of all units.

"This is war. Achievements cannot be made without sacrifice. Initially, we proposed two plans to the Central Military Commission — two scenarios. One was to capture Pratas Island from Taiwan and reclaim the Diaoyu Islands from Japan, then encircle Taiwan from the north and south, gradually applying psychological warfare over time to force the Taiwanese leadership into submission. The other was to launch a blitzkrieg to occupy Taipei before the United States could act, forcing Taiwan to submit. We intended the former to proceed with minimal casualties, but after failing to capture the main Diaoyu Island, the first plan was halted, and now even the second plan seems to have somewhat run aground. We've given the Taiwanese military time to dig in. But preparations for the landing forces are steadily underway. The sacrifices were not small. If you ask whether we are falling into the Concorde fallacy, it's not an accurate way to describe the situation; the investment can still be sufficiently recouped."

"I see. What's your opinion, Colonel Lin?"

"The former plan — which we nicknamed the 'six-month plan' — aimed to coerce Taiwan with minimal human casualties. But there were concerns with this plan from the start. If it took any longer than six months then it would be impossible to ignore the likelihood that Taiwan could secure military support from the United States.

"Personally, I thought it was impossible from the beginning. The latter plan, a short, decisive battle, was supposed to see a landing operation conducted over a week — before American public opinion was roused. Our timeline for it has now doubled, but American public opinion is still tepid. A one-week delay is unlikely to pose a significant obstacle. The Navy has suffered greatly, but our carriers are still intact. We've lost at best a third of our jet fighters, but we still outnumber the combined forces of Japan, Taiwan, and the U.S. in the Far East in raw numbers. However, there are many variables that could worsen the situation. Not just Japan's involvement; the United States could enter the conflict at any moment on the decision of the president. They've also shown that they can sink our carriers whenever they wish with pretty limited air power."

"Do you think Japan's involvement alone could force us to abandon our landing operation?"

"It comes down to air power...Japan is making steady preparations for that. But without the involvement of the United States, I assess that Japan will not engage in combat in the Taiwan Strait; it would be too much of a gamble. It's also simply too far from their bases — eight-hundred kilometres from Naha in Okinawa to the Taiwan Strait. They can't sustain a force over the Taiwan Strait with the number of air-to-air refuellers in their inventory."

"Understood. I'd like all of you here to consider this. If you were to suggest halting the operation here, you would not be held accountable. Well, it might cut off your path to promotion. However, if you advise continuing the operation as is, and it ends in failure, you *will* be held accountable. You probably won't be sent to a detention facility; if we did that, we'd need to build new ones to accommodate thousands. But you might be sent to a remote outpost without even a proper toilet, where you'd shiver from the cold every night as you try to sleep. Knowing that risk, would you still advise continuing the operation?" Pan studied the faces of everyone present, one by one.

"Sir, taking full control of Hong Kong, and finally raising the Five-star Red Flag in Taipei will be the fulfilment of the Chinese Dream. We've now secured our place in the world. China dominates the global economy. If reclaiming Taiwan lets us become the undisputed world leader in both name and substance, then what is there to hesitate about? We've already lost over three thousand troops in battle when we add up the casualties of our ground forces. If we back down here, their deaths will have been in vain!" Major General Sun made this appeal with pride.

"General Sun, that's exactly what the West calls the Concorde fallacy," replied Pan with a wry smile. "I will return to Zhongnanhai and report the situation to the Central Military Commission. You've all worked hard. Ultimatums will soon be delivered to the relevant nations. By tomorrow morning, the

Taiwanese will regret the many disrespects they have shown us. Thank you, everyone!"

Pan was present for no more than ten minutes, but his purpose for coming was clear. It was to diffuse responsibility. The operation would likely succeed. It was uncertain how many weeks it would take, but they would dye the island red with the blood of the youth and reclaim Taiwan. However, should the number of dead exceed the tolerance of the people, someone will be held responsible. By diffusing the responsibility now, it would be enough to offer up a few scapegoats when the time came. That was Pan's reason for soliciting opinions.

———

The Japan Air Self-Defense Force Air Defense Command Headquarters was located at Yokota Air Base alongside Headquarters U.S. Forces Japan. An underground passage connected the buildings of the two headquarters.

Representatives from the Ground, Maritime and Air branches were refining operational plans in the 'Abyss Room' at Air Defense Command Headquarters, a room named so as to signify 'gazing into the abyss'.

Without their mastery, defending the Senkaku Islands would have been an impossible task. Their achievements were significant. In particular, Air Self-Defense Force Lieutenant Colonel Catherine Eiko Kitagawa, with her out-of-the-box ideas and connections within the U.S. military, devised operational plans that kept them from the brink on numerous occasions.

Her father was an intelligence officer in the U.S. military who died in combat in Iraq. His subordinates from that time had safely risen to general officer ranks, some of whom were now stationed here at Yokota. Known by some within the ASDF as 'Madam Magic', she could walk through the underground passage between headquarters just by showing her face.

They dimmed the lights in the room and gathered in front of the thirty-three-inch screen to watch the program get underway. It was a combat simulation, specifically an air operations simulation. The enemy and friendly forces were divided into red and blue. The two sides clashed fiercely over the main island of Taiwan, with Blue Force gradually gaining ground and pushing the frontline of the airspace over the Taiwan Strait. However, when Blue Force's fighters reached their fuel limits, they suddenly began to turn back.

"Is this what they use at Red Flag?" asked Colonel Minemitsu Habu, the team leader of the Operations Division Special Unit at Air Defense Command Headquarters.

"Basically the same thing. I heard that it came from a group that was developing a warfare simulation video game. A defence contractor recruited the entire development team and polished it up into a military version of the program," explained Lieutenant Colonel Kitagawa.

"I think whatever parameters you've got in there correlating the increased sortie rates to the malfunction and early return rate is a bit high? The F-35s are turning back a little too much."

"Actually, this is the level of malfunction rate we're seeing. The Eagles are fully seasoned, so there are rarely cases where they have to turn back due to wear from increased sorties. We've also got them in combat air patrols protecting the P-1s."

"Even so, the performance of the F-15EX is incredible. This truly is a game-changer, comparable to stealth fighters."

Once the program pushed the enemy fighters back to the mainland coast and maintained this state for an hour. During that time, Blue Force fighters were continuously swapping in and out to refuel, but they never allowed the enemy to advance.

Habu paused the program and ordered the screen to be turned off, then stood in front of the whiteboard. The dim light made the writing on the whiteboard barely readable.

"Let's identify the problems. First, the anticipated casualties. In the most severe conditions set in the program, we lose two squadrons. That's not within acceptable level of risk. Second, boosting the number of air-to-air refuelling aircraft. We need the U.S. to agree on that. Third, deploying the Joker. If we can deploy the Joker, we can significantly reduce our own casualties, the first point. Fourth is about Amami, but…"

"The airport there is already ready, and the PAC-3 has been deployed. Offshore, we have the support of the MSDF's destroyer fleet."

"Chinese spies will be watching of course, but given the current situation where landlines, mobile phones, and the internet are down, they can only send their reports back to the mainland via shortwave radio or satellite radio."

"The fifth point concerns the extent to which our runways can survive Chinese ballistic missile attacks. If it comes to it, there's also the option of landing at bases in Taiwan, but these are likely to be heavily damaged as well."

Commander Kunihiko Fukuhara from the Systems Programs Division in the Operations and Plans Department of the Maritime Staff Office, raised his right hand to introduce another concern. "A sixth point: Suppose the PLA Navy, diminished by our attacks, decides against blue-water operations and retreats to coastal areas. If they simply hold their position, they could delay for one or two weeks. Are we able to maintain round-the-clock fighter formations over the Taiwan Strait for that time?"

Lieutenant Commander Kota Hinoue, a P-1 pilot, suggested, "Why don't you push the P-1s with escorts towards the coastal areas?"

"That's reckless. The coastline of Fujian across from Taipei is full of inlets; plenty of places for ships to hide. And we'd be targeted by land-based missiles while we're searching for the enemy ships."

"But we can still take out the large ships. This isn't World War II; we can find them in advance with reconnaissance satellites."

"Alright. We'll add that as the sixth factor. I'll go call the commander. If you have any other concerns, please add them to the list."

At the end of Habu's shift, an A4-sized envelope arrived from Intelligence Headquarters. Kitagawa signed for it and opened it up. It contained monochrome reconnaissance satellite photos. Kitagawa, who was not a pilot but an intelligence officer, stuck the infrared image photos to the board and, holding an LED lantern, compared them with previous images.

"They're totally different."

Air Defense Command Commander, Lieutenant General Takumi Maruyama, strode in wearing his flight suit. "Catherine, brief me on the images. I haven't seen them yet. Is this showing missile transport vehicles?"

"Not quite. This is near a Rocket Force base in Hunan Province, eight-hundred kilometres inland from Fujian. It's part of a road that's been widened to accommodate the passage of large Rocket Force vehicles. The images show a curve that hasn't been well maintained, where the PLA's large ten-wheeled vehicles are forced to make big steering manoeuvres. This results in noticeable tire wear and leaves unique tracks. Only the PLA's ten-wheeled vehicles leave such tracks here. By counting them, we can determine how many vehicles have recently passed through this area. The left photo shows tracks in the last three days, and the right photo is from two hours ago."

"Can't we just count the number of vehicles at the deployment site?"

"They've deployed a large number of decoy vehicles — balloons inflated to look like real vehicles — there too. This imagery of the road curve is the only place where we can accurately estimate the number of real vehicles that have been deployed."

"The tracks are completely different…The left photo shows the tracks of two or three vehicles, but the right photo here…"

"Probably more than ten vehicles have passed through."

"The U.S. is also saying that tonight's deployment is real. They're likely readying around five-hundred ballistic missiles for launch. The question is how many will be aimed at us. Even if they're conventional warheads, the fact that they're launching ballistic missiles without hesitation shows they're desperate. So, Catherine, do you think the plan is likely to succeed?"

"Yes, the introduction of the F-15EX is a game changer." Kitagawa turned on the monitor and accelerated the program to show it at a hundred times speed. "We can support Taiwan's air defence and prevent the PLA from crossing the Taiwan Strait. But there are a lot of essential conditionals…" Kitagawa placed a lantern on the table in front of the whiteboard, which listed the issues identified. Although the facility had a generator, the U.S. was the priority here, so the ASDF had to use electricity sparingly. "USAF air-to-air refuelling support is essential. Whether this is feasible or not will largely be the determining factor. That's the negotiation item…As for the potential loss of up to two squadrons, Colonel Habu, sir, I'll let you speak to that."

"Two squadrons is the result of simulations run under the strictest conditions. I reloaded the conditions ten times, but no scenario resulted in more than that."

"Is that without the *Joker*?"

"Yes, that's without deploying the Joker. If we use the Joker, we could potentially keep losses to less than one squadron."

"And then there's the matter of how many airfields can avoid damage from ballistic missile attacks. Is it just me, or does it feel like there are too many uncertainties?"

"Even if everything south of Amami is wiped out, with sorties from Nyutabaru and air-to-air refuelling alone…"

"You're joking, right? That's fifteen-hundred kilometres one way to the Taiwan Strait. That would make the Joker a go/no-go requirement."

"Yes, conversely, if we deploy the Joker, we can hold the Taiwan Strait. Also, I haven't written this here, but the Taiwanese Air Force isn't included in this plan. If Taiwan's latest F-16V fighters come under our C2, it will greatly enhance the chances of success, although we'd need to provide the fuel."

"Taiwan would cooperate to that extent if there's a high likelihood of success. I'd have to first secure a promise for tankers from the USAF, then convince the Air Chief of Staff, get a nod from the Joint Staff and the Internal Bureau, and get final sign-off from the prime minister. It looks like we can win, so let's get approval to be sent to the front line from the get-go."

"If this all happens, and we succeed, this war will end by tomorrow. After that, no one else will need to die — not the Chinese, and certainly not our SDF personnel. Japan will likely incur China's wrath, but that will be a matter for the diplomats."

"Understood. What's the status of Amami Airport?"

"Preparations for our arrival are underway. Control, maintenance, and crucially, the air-to-air refuelling units have been deployed, and the airport is protected by the Patriots."

"Good! Move the Hyakuri EX squadron forward to Amami, but do it as discreetly as possible. By the way, what about the MSDF? It seems the P-1s are taking significant risks."

Hinoue responded confidently. "We trust the ASDF will cover us. We can sink approaching ships while using Taiwan's mountains as cover. Then once it's safe, we'll move out to the strait and launch a barrage of Mavericks."

"Thank you. At the very least, we're obliged to present this plan to the Prime Minister's Office. I'll head next door to the USAF. Colonel Habu, take the sim data and a few others and head to Ichigaya to finalise things with the Air Chief of Staff. I'll follow later. If we can't get cooperation from the U.S., that's where the discussion ends. We won't escalate it to the Chief of Joint Staff or go to the Prime Minister. I'll just come back. But I expect that the USAF will at least co-operate to provide tanker support. Running a gas station in a safe rear area." The Air Defence Command Commander dashed out.

Kitagawa mused. She believed the plan was sound, but the Japanese government was notoriously indecisive and prone to procrastination. While she could perhaps persuade the uniformed Chief of Joint Staff, she worried that the plan might still be halted at the bureaucratic level within the Internal Bureau.

———

At Hualien Air Force Base in Taiwan, Major General Li Yan, who commanded the 5th Tactical Fighter Wing, stood at the lectern in front of the hangar on the apron, microphone in hand. The base was dark. A flashlight was placed at his feet, illuminating him from the chest up.

Sixty F-16 fighters of different variants were spread across three squadrons. Fifty platforms were still operational after engagements with the enemy reduced their number. Half of these F-16s were the latest F-16V variant, which possessed capabilities superior to Japan's F-15J Eagles. One squadron was always out patrolling the Taiwan Strait, so only half of the pilots and maintenance personnel were here at any given time.

"Officers and airmen! Listen here! The PLA Rocket Force is on the move. Ballistic missile attacks are imminent. This base could well be obliterated by dawn. Therefore, I'm ordering all aircraft to depart. Once we're up, we'll cycle in small groups to refuel and hold in the airspace above.

"The enemy will likely target the early warning radar on Mt. Leshan first. We can expect dozens of ballistic missiles to be aimed at that site. Once that radar is taken down, we'll have no means to detect incoming ballistic missiles. Therefore, once Leshan is out, we should assume that our base is completely destroyed. You will then follow the instructions of your formation lead and evacuate to Okinawa. Fuel will be provided by U.S. Air Force tankers; I have secured that assurance. If there's any guidance from the Japan Air Self-Defense Force, make sure to follow it. If Naha and Kadena are intact, head there. If you're concerned about fuel, you can land at Miyako or Ishigaki, although those locations are also likely to be targeted. I'm praying we don't have to ditch any of our aircraft.

"I'll be staying here in the meantime, but I'll take shelter in the underground bunker once the ballistic missile attack commences. For those of you also remaining, do not rely on the cave hangars next door at Chiashan. It's a known target and is already empty. All weapons and ammunition have been evacuated. It's likely that we'll be temporarily occupied by the enemy, but there is no need for despair. The Army will conduct delaying actions and commit to guerrilla warfare to create an opportunity for a counteroffensive. You should return when that time comes. I pray that you all fight bravely." Major General Li saluted and stepped down from the podium, the pilots then raced to their beloved aircraft.

"Sir, you won't evacuate with us?" asked Lieutenant Colonel Liu Jianhong, who led the 17th Flying Squadron. "An underground bunker is hardly reassuring."

"I know. But the commander can't just run away as the base air defence holds its ground, especially with lodgers from the missile defence units here. How many ballistic missiles do you think they'll fire onto us?"

"It won't be fifty; maybe twenty or thirty. The cave hangars are an irritant, and the massive base on the other side of the mountains is a prime target."

"Copy. But even if ballistic missiles punch holes in the runway, we can have it operational again in half a day. There's a limit to what two or three dozen missiles can do. The big kicker will be cruise missiles. With ballistic missiles, we have the Patriot PAC-3 and Sky Bow 3 systems. Our air defence missile network is the second densest in the world after Israel's. There'll be some that get through, but you don't need to worry about that. A base can always be restored; we have units on standby for that. You know, the Office of the President and Air Force Command have ordered that Hualien must be held at all costs."

"Impossible. Absolutely impossible!"

"I think so too, but we need a base for counterattacks, and a location to draw enemy fire. Hualien here on the eastern side of the mountains is ideally situated for that."

"Even so, it can't be held; not without help from Japan and the U.S. I think it would be wiser to abandon everything for now and have all units evacuate."

"Yes. But having just one fighter base intact can give people hope. You don't need to take unnecessary risks. Don't worry about the cruise missiles or the follow on fighters. Just get out quickly. That's an order."

"Yes, sir. We'll do that. I pray for your safety!" The two exchanged a firm handshake as the fighters formed up and took off.

Major General Li stood at attention at the edge of the apron and saluted the departing fighters.

———

It wasn't only Air Force units that were trying to evacuate. AH-64E Apache Guardian attack helicopter units at the Taiwanese Army's 601st Aviation Brigade in Taoyuan City, southwest of Taipei, were also taking off. In the dimly lit hangar, Major General General Fu Xiangren of the Taiwanese Army was giving a final briefing to his helicopter pilots who were about to depart.

"Officers and soldiers, intel reports are telling us that ballistic missile launches are imminent. They will strike here within just five minutes of detection. Intel is also telling us that across the strait, PLA soldiers and marine forces are embarking on naval ships and civilian ferries. Once they leave the shore, travelling at twenty knots, they'll reach our coast in about four to six hours. By then, we will likely have lost control of the airspace over this territory. We'll have no role to play.

"You all will evacuate per the procedures and head to your respective aircraft concealment and evacuation locations. Part of the maintenance element has already departed. After all aircraft have launched, the remaining maintenance teams will follow across land routes. A time will come when your fighting power will be needed again. It could be next week or it could be in six months. Even if spider webs form on the engines, endure! Hide your aircraft, subsist on whatever you can, protect the fuel and weapons, and wait for the time to counterattack. We *will* counterattack and drive out the enemy. Now, go!"

Major Ping Longyi, Commanding Officer of the 1st Attack Squadron, brought a new gunner pilot to Captain Lan Zhiling. He and Lan had flown combat missions over the Diaoyu Islands together to prevent the PLA from establishing an island foothold to the northeast of Taiwan. Second Lieutenant Tian Zuyi was a rookie officer, having been in flight school for just six months.

Captain Lan, the public face of the Taiwan Army's new recruitment efforts, was teaming up with a fellow female pilot for the first time. But this one was a rookie. Lan had been so preoccupied with her own duties that she had never had to mentor anyone else before. Her previous front seat gunner had been injured from the impact when they were shot down; although he survived, he was still in the hospital. Taiwan Marine Corps troops had sacrificed their lives to rescue them at the Diaoyu Islands.

"Since there won't be much to do at the evacuation site, I'll get you to study up. If we can get a power source, we can also practice in training mode."

"Great! I'm lucky to be paired with a superior who has the skills, knowledge, and good looks that you do."

Tian reminded Lan of her own freshness when she first joined the Army. "The battlefield isn't as glamorous as you might think...But it's not common to get a new aircraft the day after surviving being shot down."

"Captain Lan," interrupted Major Ping, "we'll have to evacuate to a location somewhat distant. Obviously two helos will require quite a bit of space. For comms between us, instead of using radios, we'll likely have to send messages by motorcycle or bicycle. Protecting the helos is our top priority." Major Ping and Captain Lan had been through life-and-death situations together around the Diaoyu Islands. Lan considered herself lucky to be able to fly with him again.

"How long do you think it'll take before we can launch a counterattack, sir?" Tian asked.

"Well, it won't be in less than a week. The battle for Taipei will unfold first, and the ground forces are expected to initially withdraw while they can still mount an organised resistance. During that time, we'll wait for international opinion to rouse... At the very least, it'll take two weeks, perhaps even a month. I hope it doesn't stretch to six months…parts might start to get rusty, and the engines may no longer start. Stay safe, Tian, and study hard. If we get a chance, we'll have a stealthy welcome party for you, maybe cook up some rats in a pot. If the wait drags on, food supplies will probably deteriorate that much. Be prepared. Hunger will start clouding our thinking the day after we arrive in location."

The hiding places for both helicopters would likely be about twenty to thirty kilometres apart. They wouldn't be able to communicate easily.

"Also, be careful around the locals. If we start losing and falling into disadvantageous situations, there will definitely be traitors. After landing, hide the helos so that not even the locals can find them."

"Understood. Stay safe, sir."

They saluted and headed toward their respective helicopters. Captain Lan's eyes welled up with tears. Similar farewells must be happening at air bases across all of Taiwan, now in a state of blackout. She couldn't help but wonder, do we have a chance of winning?

———

The Air Defense Command Headquarters contingent landed on the helipad at the Ministry of Defense building in Ichigaya, Tokyo. Thirty minutes later, the helicopter carrying Lieutenant General Maruyama landed and they joined up, then proceeded on to the Prime Minister's Office, escorted by police cars.

They were shocked to see the very heart of the capital plunged into darkness. The occasional lights they could see were from convenience stores, guidance lights held by uniformed police officers, or the red flashing lights of patrol cars. Riot police had been deployed to secure the roads between the National Diet Building and the Prime Minister's Office. The area around the Diet was effectively closed to traffic.

What was even more shocking was the lack of lights at the Prime Minister's Office. Chemical lights were strewn about the hallways. The ASDF contingent initially assumed they would be headed to the situation room in the basement, but it turned out that it wasn't in use because of the lack of electricity. They were forced to climb the emergency stairs to reach the Prime Minister's Executive Office. As they approached the fifth floor, the strong smell of cigar smoke wafted through the air.

"Lieutenant Commander Hinoue, don't you have a proper uniform?"

"This flight suit is my uniform. It's wartime now; no time to fuss over wearing different uniforms, even if we are meeting the prime minister."

"I'd prefer wearing my flight suit too; it's more comfortable." Lieutenant General Maruyama led the climb up the stairs. He was beginning to regret leaving Habu in Ichigaya. There were a number of issues needing coordination back there at the Ministry of Defense, and Habu was the only one who could be entrusted with them. Still, Maruyama wished Habu was by his side heading to this political battlefield.

Upon reaching the fifth floor, the Deputy Chief Cabinet Secretary and the Senior Deputy Minister for Foreign Affairs were waiting for them. After a quick situation briefing that took just thirty seconds, Senior Deputy Minister for Foreign Affairs Katakura led them into the open door of the Prime Minister's Executive Office.

Prime Minister Aso was sitting deeply in his chair, resting his head against the backrest as if asleep. The room was dimly lit, with several LED lanterns scattered about, but they were insufficiently bright. These lanterns were designed for camping, mimicking the flicker of flames.

"Do you folks know what time it is now?"

"It's two in the morning, sir. We apologise."

"Have the missiles been launched?"

"We have no such information yet."

"Looking at those camping lanterns, it really feels like I'm being sucked in. I had them taken away earlier, but weirdly, I realised they calmed my mind so I had them brought back...So, have you brought any uplifting news?"

"We have an operational plan that might end this war before the PLA lands tomorrow."

"Does the fact that an ASDF three-star has come to brief me mean this is primarily an air combat operation?"

"Yes, sir. It's an interdiction operation using fighters and patrol aircraft. We've just received the latest model of the F-15 fighter jet, the F-15EX, from the U.S. We immediately deployed them for the defence of the Senkaku Islands and achieved remarkable results. Just four of these fighters shot down forty enemy aircraft. The most significant feature of this fighter is its weapons capacity. It can carry twice the number of air-to-air missiles than our early model Eagles. If we can keep these fighters airborne for extended periods, we believe we can prevent an enemy push."

Maruyama signalled Lieutenant Colonel Kitagawa to take out the twenty-one-inch tablet from her briefcase and play the simulation video. Prime Minister Aso reluctantly put on his reading glasses and focused on the screen.

"By continuously rotating a force of two-hundred friendly fighters to maintain presence over Taiwan, we can completely repel Chinese military aircraft. Meanwhile, MSDF patrol aircraft that have pushed down to the eastern side of Taiwan's Central Mountain Range will attack the enemy's naval forces with long-range anti-ship missiles and sweep them away. If, after that, any landing forces still attempt to approach, they'll be sunk using short-range Maverick missiles. The Chinese landing forces will then have to choose between annihilation or withdrawal."

"Oh? Fighting eight-hundred kilometres from Naha?"

"Yes, that's why we need a large number of air-to-air refuelling aircraft. The U.S. military has promised to arrange as many tankers as they can gather, including those from the U.S. Navy."

"If I may ask, I've been told over the past five years or so that the military balance in East Asia has completely shifted. Japan, or rather the Air Self-Defense Force, has completely lost its superiority, and I was told that Japan could no longer win an air battle against China. Was that information false?"

"No, in terms of the number of advanced aircraft, China clearly had the edge over us. But the situation has changed over the last two weeks. During that period, we managed to significantly reduce the number of Chinese fighters, likely to about two-thirds their original number. We are still at a disadvantage, but now we have the F-15EX. While the F-35's stealth capabilities are remarkable, the F-15EX is a true game-changer. In its first engagement, a rookie female pilot, flying just one of these planes, shot down nearly ten enemy fighters. In an instant she rewrote the kill score for ASDF pilots."

"Hmm. And what would our losses look like?"

"At most, we could lose up to two squadrons, nearly fifty aircraft. But if we bring the Taiwanese Air Force fighters under our C2 and deploy the F-35B — the carrier-based variant which has not yet been used in combat — we're confident we can keep that number to less than half."

"But there'll still be casualties, right? If a single patrol aircraft goes down, that's, what, ten MSDF sailors dead, isn't it?"

Hinoue stepped forward. "Sir, we are aware of the risks involved."

"Will this really work? Because when I was in a meeting downstairs just now, your Chief of Staff didn't mention anything like this. It was all about what happens after the PLA occupies Taipei."

"At that time, this plan didn't even exist. We have, I guess, a habit of pessimism, and we didn't believe that we could actually win by going head-to-head with the PLA's fighters."

"How many fighters does the PLA have left?"

"If we limit it to the newer models, about seven-hundred. Suppose five-hundred of those come at us."

"So we have less than half their number."

"We can win. We have early warning aircraft and stealth fighters on our side too."

"Katakura, are your thoughts?"

"Well...how significant would the losses we inflict on the PLA be?"

"The numbers would include the shot-down fighter jets plus the destroyed combat and amphibious ships. A single assault landing ship carries between two to three thousand troops. Depending on when the PLA decides to pull back, the losses could be at least twenty thousand, and possibly exceed forty thousand. But those losses would prevent the casualties associated with an occupation of Taiwan. If it comes to a battle for Taipei, the civilian casualties alone could exceed one-hundred thousand, with a similar number of troops from both sides likely to die."

"Is it right to reduce the PLA soldiers to sea debris to prevent those casualties? The U.S. once thought along these lines as well — believing that using atomic bombs was justified to reduce the casualties of a mainland Japan invasion. What to do, indeed…" The prime minister fell silent, hands clasped together as if in prayer on the desk. It was a prolonged silence, as if he might fall asleep right there. "You know, the power generator here at the Prime Minister's Office uses a gas turbine engine. The turbine itself is made by a domestic manufacturer; it's quiet and fuel-efficient. But the system as a whole uses many Chinese-made parts. In normal times, you'd just send an order form over, and the parts would arrive in about three weeks, but that's not possible now. The manufacturer would have to go around to a big hospital or somewhere that had the same machine and maybe beg them to shut down their generators to take parts for here. That'd be rather inconvenient for them, given they're saving lives. Then how would they even bring those parts here when the trains are stopped and the petrol stations are empty?

"After this war over, we must quickly improve our relations with China. There was no need to land the Amphibious Brigade on Uotsuri Island. We could have just sent fighters to drop loads of bombs or used naval gunfire to turn the island into a barren mound and annihilate them. But you see, just because we can annihilate China doesn't mean we should. They're an opponent we need to defeat moderately and let go gently. You might say that this is too lenient, especially when the lives of SDF personnel are at stake. But that's the reality of international politics. To turn them into sea debris within half a day and then rebuild Sino-Japanese relations would be…difficult.

"I am grateful for your dedication and effort. The battle for the Senkaku Islands was indeed a precarious struggle. Without your selfless dedication, pushed to the limit, we couldn't have reclaimed that island. As a politician, no amount of thanks can suffice for what you've done.

"In the future, when this war is over, I'll remember this interaction with you. I'll tell myself that had I accepted your proposal then, on that day, the losses on our side would have been limited to just twenty aircraft and their crew. Instead, the result was thousands of Ground Self-Defense Force casualties. However, I probably won't regret my decision.

"Thank you all. I have fully understood the proposal. If Japan enters the war and ground forces are cornered, this plan might come back into play. Keep it warm until then."

Maruyama stopped Hinoue as he went to speak. "Thank you, Prime Minister, for your time. It's greatly appreciated." He saluted and left the room.

Everyone thought it was a good plan. It wasn't that they were at fault, nor was it particularly inhumane. But considering political risks, it was politically untenable. Maruyama appreciated that the problem wasn't with the plan. Taiwan was likely to face a difficult path, and Japan may become involved as well; such a development was probably unavoidable.

Prime Minister Aso removed his reading glasses and placed them on the dark desk. He sighed and then asked Katakura, standing in the darkness, "Was that a mistake?"

"No. Whether it was a wise decision or not aside, it was a difficult one. We will likely face criticism questioning whether allowing Taipei to turn into a pile of rubble can be considered the right decision, but our motto is 'exclusively defensive'. In view of this national policy, that operational plan might have been somewhat of a deviation."

"Yes...But we should keep it on hold. Tighten it up and make it ready for resubmission at any time. I'll be resented for this... they'll call me a coward."

"They are professionals. They understand the political limits. I'll convey your words of encouragement to them later."

"Domon will complain when he finds out. Something about the SDF being a luxurious force that can choose its battles." Prime Minister Aso picked up an LED lantern, and for a moment, let himself be absorbed by its quiet flickering, reminiscent of a candle flame in the wind.

6

Ultimatum

The 10,250-tonne *Maya* Aegis destroyer was positioned three-hundred kilometres out at sea on a line of bearing between Naha and Taipei, prepared for ballistic missile attacks from the continent. By maintaining this position, she could respond if the enemy attempted attacks on Ishigaki or Miyako Island before also reaching Naha. Three other Aegis ships also were deployed to protect Naha.

Escort Flotilla 1 Commanding Officer Rear Admiral Shunji Kunishima had retired to his cabin and was lying down in his coveralls when the alarm sounded on the ship. He rushed back to the Flag Information Centre where a panoramic view of the continental coastline was displayed across a long monitor. Taiwan was depicted at the left end of the display, with the smaller Hainan Island behind it. The Korean Peninsula was at the right end. The coastline was shown in a curved layout, as if viewed from orbit through a fisheye lens. On the display, dozens of tracks had begun to ascend from deep within the continent. By the time Admiral Kunishima had sat down, the number of tracks exceeded one-hundred.

"It doesn't seem to be a simultaneous time-on-target impact attack."

"Seems not, sir. But with this number of missiles, simultaneous ToT is probably not necessary." Chief of Staff Captain Tokuhiro Umehara, who had just been warming the seat, observed how the Aegis system was predicting the paths of each ballistic missile, projecting the estimated trajectories in front of their actual ballistic paths.

Missile after missile continued to rise. The count had now surpassed three-hundred. Most of them seemed likely to impact Taiwan's main island. Above Taiwan, the fighters that had been patrolling the airspace had begun to gradually draw back. Some were heading in the direction of Okinawa, even though the Japanese government still hadn't decided whether it would receive them.

"Were there any notifications about this?"

"No, I haven't heard anything. The ASDF planes will probably take off, though. Looks like they're also heading this way."

Impact time was imminent. There was no time to hesitate. Friendly aircraft had begun taking off from Naha Airport. The slower patrol planes turned directly out to sea. The more powerful fighters climbed straight up; some were even taking off from the taxiways. Coast Guard planes and prefectural police helicopters also took off during this time. The aircraft had already been in place and ready to take off within five minutes of ballistic missile launches.

"How many missiles are headed for Naha?"

"Roughly five-hundred have now been launched. With this many, there shouldn't be a second wave. About thirty are headed for Naha, and the same number for Kadena. It's a bit more than last time."

"That's too much for *Haguro* alone! Direct *Haguro* to prepare for engagement in defence of Naha and Kadena! Three ship defence!"

"Even with three ships, intercepting sixty missiles is impossible!"

"We've got nothing else. The Patriots will have to take care of the rest. And this ship is going to have to abandon Ishigaki. Unfortunate, but that airport is just in the middle of fields. This ship is only to intercept missiles targeting the Miyako Islands; Miyako Island and Shimoji Island only! Expend all missiles if necessary, but fire them one at a time. Let's trust in the capabilities of the SM-3 Block IIA missiles."

"Sir, I just realised. We can still defend Ishigaki. The attack on the Miyako Islands will likely be concentrated on Shimoji Island. There's no point in attacking the fifteen-hundred metre runway Miyako Island itself. The enemy will want to destroy the three-thousand metre runway on Shimoji Island."

"That's a gamble. What if it fails? One could fall on a residential area."

"Half of the residents have already evacuated the island. Besides, the missile warning alarms should be sounding. There shouldn't be anyone around the airport."

"Understood. Abandon Miyako Airport! Focus on Ishigaki Airport and Shimoji Island. Do you think EOR is feasible?"

"Engage-on-remote? If we have any spare missiles, we can use at least one on *Haguro*'s guidance. Engage any missiles coming directly at us with the shorter range SM-6s; that'll let us share more SM-3s with *Haguro*."

"Aye-aye, over to the intercept control officer."

The screen had already turned completely white. Around Taiwan alone, over four-hundred military aircraft were attempting to evacuate, all tracking northeast, towards Okinawa. At Naha Airport, measures had been put in place to prevent the numerous Ground, Maritime, and Air Self-Defense Force aircraft from having to remain on standby, but despite this, forty aircraft were still waiting to take off.

"The government shouldn't have ignored this; they should have coordinated with the Taiwanese in advance. Way too many aircraft to handle without proper air traffic control."

Missiles began hitting targets in Taiwan. First, the naval bases, and then the military airfields. Some army barracks also seemed to be targeted, but there appeared to be no missiles aimed directly at Taipei itself. The *Maya* then started to launch her SM-3 Block IIA missiles to intercept mid-course.

Haguro was positioned north of *Maya*, closer to the main island of Okinawa. *Maya* launched her remaining missiles which were remotely guided by *Haguro* for intercept.

———

Domon was face down on the table, snoring loudly. The mobile connection with the mainland was down, so there were no missile warning alerts via broadcast signal. However, he was awakened by the roaring sound and red exhaust of a missile launched by the nearby PAC-3 unit as it soared into the sky.

Someone inside the Administration building was blowing a whistle, calling for an evacuation. Machida and his colleagues quickly packed up their gear and started tossing it into the large basket.

"Has there been any contact?"

"No, nothing. But the drone footage showed one of the destroyers that was trying to enter the port turn her rudder and head out to sea. Also, that rotor noise is from an Okinawa Prefectural Police Agusta helicopter. Everyone is evacuating from the airport all at once."

"Hurry up and get in the vehicle! Get on with it! Squad leaders, make sure you do a headcount! Leave anything non-essential behind." Domon went outside and headed towards a large truck. Machida and others followed him. "How long have we got?"

"About ninety seconds!"

"Alright, get those vehicles moving!" Domon got into the passenger side of a Type 73 truck. The driver floored the accelerator, completely ignoring the base speed limit. At the front gate, riot police were dragging the sit-down protestors out of the way. "What the hell are they doing! Run!" he shouted.

The main target was probably Naha Airport, where units of the three SDF branches were deployed. We managed somehow last time, he thought. This time will be harder.

————

Captain Lan Zhiling piloted her Apache Guardian one-hundred kilometres south through the mountainous region, then briefly out to the eastern side of the island, a manoeuvre intended to deceive radars on the continent. After that, she landed it on a riverbed in the Wanda River valley region. Rocks kicked up, potentially damaging the aircraft, but there were no other clear areas around here.

After shutting the systems down, she and her rookie gunner, Second Lieutenant Tian Ziyu, disembarked onto the riverbank. She chose this spot because it was unlikely to flood, even with some rain. Still, she would be sure to check the next morning in case she ought to change the landing position slightly.

Once outside, Lan looked up into the night sky. It was filled with stars. During her time on Diaoyu Island, the weather had been persistently poor, and she had not had the opportunity to witness such a starry night.

The maintainers were waiting, and they immediately draped a camouflage net over the helicopter.

"Beautiful, isn't it?" Tian was also looking up at the night sky. They were over a thousand metres above sea level here; the air was clear. But because they were in a valley, they couldn't see far. The mountains obscured the view, completely hiding the coastline.

They heard the sound of a fighter passing overhead. Soon after, there was a bright flash in the eastern direction. It was like lightning flashing in the distance. "Where was that?"

"Probably the Hualien and Chiashan Air Force Bases. The mainland would want to destroy those particularly annoying bases the most. Chiashan base, three kilometres from Hualien towards the mountains, has those huge hangars built into caves in the mountainside. That's all I really know though."

The sky lit up again. Flashes then continued at irregular intervals. Second Lieutenant Tian began counting them. "Did you see that flash! That means the intercept was successful, right?"

"I wonder if a Sky Bow got it?"

Tian counted five explosions in the sky all up, but it was hard to tell whether these were successful intercepts. Hualien was at least forty kilometres from here. Although they could see the light, they couldn't hear the sound of the impact. They were likely one-tonne warheads, which would result in a considerable explosion. The shockwaves would hit buildings within a five-hundred metre radius. Flying debris would move at the speed of bullets, turning into lethal projectiles.

Bases across the whole country would have been hit. The flashing lights finally ceased.

"Fifteen missiles, including those that exploded in the air."

"Now for the cruise missiles."

"Is there anything we can do?"

"No. The radio's not working either, so all we can do is sleep through it."

Sleeping tents should have been pitched nearby. Since they were in a valley region there was plenty of water around, and ablutions wouldn't be a problem.

"Don't go near the water to wash your hands, and definitely don't drink it."

"Is there something wrong with it?"

"Echinococcus. Over ten years it can consume your liver and kill you."

"Oh, right. I grew up in Taipei. I don't have much knowledge about survival skills. Please keep teaching me, Captain."

"Hey, I'm a city girl too…"

What a situation to be in, thought Lan. Just when she'd barely made it back alive from that uninhabited Japanese island… she hoped this life in the mountains didn't drag on. There was probably not much food left in the village down the mountain. She prayed they wouldn't have to hide out like this for any more than a week. And as the highest-ranking officer there, she had to take command of the maintenance troops.

Domon heard the sound of a Patriot missile launching from behind his departing truck. Flames scorched the night sky. The sit-down protesters seemed to finally accept the situation at the sight of this and got up all at once and started running. Missiles exploded in the sky. Domon figured they were probably those that the Aegis ships had intercepted, causing them to miss their intended targets. It was unclear how many had fallen.

"Garu, you still got the drone up?"

"Yes, sir. It's still up. There are impacts at Naha Airport! Three or four of them. The last one was big."

They were only three kilometres from Naha Airport and they could hear the sound of the impacts.

"Once things ease up, we'll turn our focus onto disaster recovery. We're the closest unit to the affected area that's capable of doing anything."

"Yes, sir. We'll prepare for the all-clear."

The truck convoy slowed down, deliberately moving at a crawl. After confirming that there were no impacts at Camp Naha, Domon ordered them to head to Naha Airport. They could see fire in several places, but the damage seemed minimal based on the footage from the drone that Machida was operating.

———

Lieutenant Colonel Keiko Togawa, Deputy Commander of the Airborne Warning and Control Wing's Airborne Warning and Surveillance Group, was aboard a Boeing E-767 Airborne Warning and Control System aircraft, flying over the waters west of Amami Oshima. Her immediate task was to safely guide formations of F-15EX fighters that had taken off from Hyakuri Air Base to Amami Oshima Airport for landing.

There was no power outage on Amami Oshima, but a blackout had been enforced at the airport. Even though the F-15EXs were equipped with excellent optical sensors, which reduced concerns about their landing capabilities, the runway lights were turned on as they approached for landing.

Just as the first formation began their approach to land, a ballistic missile alert was issued. It was probably initiated by the U.S. military stationed at the Mt. Leshan early warning radar site on Taiwan or an associated unit. The site was essentially under American control, and rumour had it that data feeds from the radar, which could peer deep into the mainland, were sent directly to the Americans in real-time. This was not particularly surprising. Moments later, the number of contacts on her display multiplied rapidly. At the same time, Taiwanese military aircraft started retreating towards the Okinawa area.

"It's irresponsible to expect us to handle this at the unit level," Togawa grumbled.

"What should we do about this many?" Major Taiji Uchimura, the deputy commander of the 602nd Squadron, was also at a loss.

"We need to verify the safety of our bases and the airstrips on the remote islands first. Once that's confirmed, the aircraft with longer ranges should head to Okinawa's main island, and those with shorter ranges should land at the airports on the remote islands. Let's also establish comms with the Taiwanese Air Force's E-2K Hawkeye. But first and foremost, we need to confirm the safety of each airfield."

Despite some misses, the Aegis ships performed well. At the very least, they managed to protect Ishigaki and the Miyako Islands as intended. Kadena, the priority for protection, was still undamaged. Naha Airport did receive a number of hits, but the runways were mostly unscathed. Just clearing the surface would be sufficient for aircraft to land. Three missiles had also fallen into the water between the two runways.

While coordinating with the Taiwanese Air Force, the radars on two Aegis ships detected a belated ballistic missile launched. It was not tracking towards the Ryukyu Islands but towards Kyushu on Japan's mainland. The target was unclear. After disappearing from the Aegis radars, ASDF radar sites began tracking it. The missile entered the atmosphere over Osaka and then started following an erratic trajectory, swaying left and right, its altitude also varying irregularly.

"That's not a DF-17? What the hell is it...?"

It was a hypersonic glide vehicle and it was heading towards the capital, Tokyo. PAC-3 units were deployed in Ichigaya. They were the only option available to intercept the HGV.

———

Standing at the entrance of the convenience store as dawn was about to break, Minami Komachi was dealing with local customers — the 'victims' of the current situation. It had been a busy night, but then she remembered that saying: *Every night has its dawn.* A foreign student once mentioned that this was their favourite Japanese saying. At that time, she merely nodded nonchalantly, knowing there was such a thing as a night without dawn. She recalled when that cold, snowy night was about to break into dawn, only to reveal that her world was no more...

Minami and her colleagues took turns in resting. The volunteers really worked hard. She didn't want to admit it, but it really was a classy neighbourhood. The people really were virtuous and kind.

At dawn, a neighbour brought over a pot of hot coffee which everyone gratefully received in paper cups from the coffee maker. It was a moment of revival. Once dawn broke, the first task would be to settle the day's pay for all the volunteers. She planned to wake up the proprietress, have her go home to change clothes, and then head home before noon to catch some sleep.

Given the continuing power outage, she couldn't take the train to university. Classes would likely be cancelled anyway. She figured she would take a nap and then start her shift again in the evening. A fax sent from headquarters mentioned that part-time workers who took shifts under these circumstances would receive a special allowance.

The crowd around the convenience store had thinned out considerably, but there were still people sitting on the ground, leaning against the convenience store windows, sleeping. Minami thought they were fortunate. Having these lights in the neighbourhood, they could avoid the fear of darkness. Sitting at a table, sipping coffee, she took a bite from a biscuit that a neighbour had brought over. Yasu sat down beside her and brought up the topic of help wanted. Apparently a nearby convenience store hadn't recruited volunteer staff on-site, and they had asked him a few times for help. The pay for these shifts would be higher.

"What will you do? You must be tired after working all night. It's my duty of care to make sure you don't push yourself."

"No, I'll go. I need the money. If the power comes back, I'll finish in the evening. If the blackout continues, I'll take a break and then come back here tonight. I need to earn while I can."

"Why are you saving up so much money? What do you want to do with it?"

"I'm not really sure. I really want to start a business, but I don't actually know what kind of business."

"That's cool, but a bit strange…"

"What about you, Miss Minami? You don't talk much about yourself, do you?"

"Why do you think that? You've always worked the day shift, and I'm always in the evenings, so we barely have any overlapping hours."

"That's just what Miss Keiko said. She mentioned that you don't really talk about yourself."

"Ah, that's because — just between you and me — Keiko is a total chatterbox. During breaks, she talks non-stop, like a machine gun, all by herself. Anyone with her hardly gets a word in edgeways."

"Ah, I know what you mean."

Looking up at the sky, Minami thought she saw a shooting star. At first, it seemed to be a shooting star, but soon after, there were flashes high in the sky, like fireworks. It happened once, then twice, three times, and then a fourth.

"What's that…?"

"Too high for fireworks. Could it be a meteorite?"

Other people around had also noticed and were looking up at the sky. The next moment, it suddenly felt like the glare of car headlights flashed across their cheeks. Then, a heavy, booming sound resonated deep in their stomachs.

Someone shouted, "Earthquake!" prompting everyone to stand up. After a delay following the initial impact sound, a wave — whether it was a shockwave or simply a sound — reverberated through. It felt as if the sound had rushed through their bodies.

Minami stood up too, and at that moment, the shockwave hit her. She instinctively covered her face as a wall-like barrage of air hit her repeatedly. This was no earthquake — it was something entirely different.

All visibility was momentarily lost. Even the light from the sign board at the front of the store was blocked. Her eyes filled with dust and she was seized by a vague anxiety that it might have been some kind of bomb blast. The strong wind seemed to carry everything away with it, and the shelves with stacked papers toppled over in dramatic fashion.

She couldn't move an inch until the wind subsided. Dust and debris flew into her mouth. Papers and paper cups spread out on the table were blown away. The wind then began to blow in the opposite direction. Once it finally subsided, her hair, mouth, and eyes were full of dust, and she was unable to move for some time.

"Is anyone hurt? Has anyone been injured?" Yasu called out. "Are you alright, Miss Minami?"

"I'm not really okay, but I'm not hurt for now. What was that? A gas explosion or something?"

"It felt like that. But I don't know where it happened. There's no wind today, so this dust isn't settling easily. Even with a flashlight on, I can't see more than five metres ahead."

Blinking her eyes to clear away the dust, Minami took a flashlight and walked around the store, calling to customers. Pieces of rubbish littered the ground, blown in from all round the place. After that, she stood paralyzed by the disaster scene in front of the store. She had to gather the scattered papers and right the fallen shelves.

A man wearing a sweatshirt with an LED band on his left arm for jogging ran in. This area was popular for early morning joggers. Even at times like this, some people don't skip their daily routines. "I need a first aid kit!" he yelled.

"Are you hurt?"

"No, not me. I also need water, a lot of clean water in plastic bottles."

"That was a gas explosion just now, right?"

"No, it was a missile. A ballistic missile! The SDF tried to intercept it with Patriots but failed, and it hit nearby."

"A ballistic missile? Is that like a nuclear bomb?"

"Not nuclear. We would have been vaporised if it were. That was a conventional warhead, about five-hundred kilos. It would have destroyed every block around it. We need to go help. It'll take forever for ambulances to get in there."

"Are you in the SDF?"

"No, my apologies. My name's Saionji. I'm a UN official from the UN Office for Disarmament Affairs. I'm back on leave.

Anyway, I need fresh water and a first aid kit, please." Saionji then picked up a handheld megaphone that was lying at his feet.

"If you can move and are wearing proper shoes, please join me! A missile has fallen nearby, and there is likely significant damage. If you've got the physical strength and are prepared to see blood please come. Bring a flashlight and bottles of fresh water!"

Minami took the emergency kit from behind the cash register. She decided to fill empty plastic bottles with water from the sink.

"What is the water for?" she asked Saionji as she stepped outside.

"Everyone's covered in dust. We need the water to wash off injuries and rinse our eyes."

"Okay, everyone. Clean the plastic bottles and fill them with water. Yasu, please clean up the shop."

"Will do. Please be careful."

Even with the flashlight pointed straight ahead, visibility was still only five or six metres.

"Make sure no one gets lost," said Saionji. "The roads might disappear from sight any moment now. If you feel disoriented, stay put until the smoke from the blast clears. Let's go!"

"You seem well accustomed to this kind of situation."

"Yes, unfortunately. I've seen my share of battlefields — Iraq, Afghanistan, Lebanon, Sudan. I took vacations to get away from battlefields."

As they moved forward, the smoke grew thicker. The sound of helicopters could be heard overhead, but it was unlikely that they could see the ground. Gradually, though, dawn began to break. This was a relief. But then a man in pyjamas, his face eerily white, suddenly appeared. Minami's heart nearly stopped. He was barefoot, and his pyjamas were torn in several places resembling a character from a zombie movie. Someone in their group gasped at the sight. They asked him if he was okay, but he didn't respond.

"He might have burst eardrums or be in shock," said Saionji. "Someone, help carry him back to the convenience store. Give him some water to drink and try to calm him down." He then called out through a megaphone, "Is anyone there? If you need help, make a loud noise! Bang on something nearby to signal us!"

Slowly, visibility improved. But the neighbourhood was gone. The residential area had completely vanished. Houses were on fire. Helicopters were now overhead, and there was hope that fire trucks would soon arrive. The ground where the road once lay was now littered with broken glass and wood debris.

Minami suddenly felt breathless. Her body started to tremble, and she had no choice but to stop. Her face turned pale, and she stood there, dazed.

"Are you alright?" Saionji asked. "If it's too much, you should sit down here. If you keep standing, you might get dizzy and fall. Sit here."

Minami shut her eyes. "I'm sorry, I can't stay here. I'm going back!" She turned on her heel and started to head back. She had no idea which way to go, but if she aimed for the opposite direction, she would hit a small stream. From there, she could find her way back to the store.

Sirens began to sound from afar. Fire engines and ambulances were arriving at last. When she reached the store, Minami saw the man from earlier sitting in a daze, attended by Yasu.

"Are you okay?" Yasu asked her.

Minami shook her head. She felt like she was on the verge of hyperventilating. Sirens from fire engines were coming from all directions. The sound of helicopters was getting louder; it wasn't just one or two — there seemed to be five or six or even more in the air.

An hour passed. Minami had been sitting in a chair, lost in thought, when the rescue group that had gone out finally returned. The white shirt that one of them was wearing was now covered with dust and had spots of blood on it. A young rescuer reported that they had managed to pull three people from the rubble, but one hadn't made it.

When Saionji returned, his hands were completely black. He asked if he could use the restroom. Minami finally stood up and showed him to the back. She offered him a nutritional drink from behind the counter, intended for the staff.

"My name is Terumi Saionji," he said. "I'm sorry for earlier. I should have noticed the change in your demeanour. I've seen it many times on the battlefield. That wasn't just a reaction to temporary shock. That looked like a post-traumatic stress response, probably from experiences in your childhood."

In a faint voice, Minami murmured, "I was the only one who survived. My family was all swept away by the tsunami."

"I'm sorry for your loss. I hope you find a way to enjoy life, not just for yourself but for your family too."

"Yes, I'm studying distribution economics."

"Really? Are you interested in the UN?" Saionji smiled.

"I'm not that great a student."

"The UN isn't just for the outstanding individuals; it's a place for those with ambition. And since Japan has fallen on hard times, the pay is better than a senior position at the Ministry of Foreign Affairs. You should look into it, should you feel inclined."

"Yes, thank you very much."

After finishing his drink, Saionji resumed his jogging pace and left.

Not everyone can live a life like that, thought Minami. I'm just an ordinary person. I've lived everyday hoping to lead a thoroughly ordinary life. I never once thought of living for my dead family. I've just been living with those memories sealed away.

———

Prime Minister Aso was in his office, watching a live feed from a Tokyo Fire Department helicopter. There was a gaping hole in a residential area, about ten metres deep and fifty metres in diameter. The blast had blown away the houses around its perimeter as well.

An official from the Ministry of Internal Affairs and Communications reported matter-of-factly the scale of the damage. Based on the aerial images and the residential district map, sixty houses were completely destroyed and two-hundred damaged. The exact number of casualties wasn't clear yet, but twenty bodies had been recovered so far, and the number was expected to rise as rescuers searched through more collapsed houses. The crater had already begun to fill with rising groundwater.

Aso turned off the monitor and cleared the room. "Do you remember years back when that newspaper copped flack for writing, 'If it's just one missile, it might be a misfire'? What's Beijing saying now?"

"They're saying it was indeed off-target. That the intended target was the riverbed. And they express their regrets," replied Katakura, the only remaining MOFA official.

"I'm no boffin, but I'm aware of the concept of 'circular error probable'. The CEP of modern nuclear missiles is just a few dozen metres. They fly thousands of kilometres with only a few dozen metres of deviation. But this missile, it seems to have missed the Tama River by more than a kilometre."

"The Defense Ministry explained that glide vehicles are still under development everywhere, and achieving such accuracy is currently impossible."

"The proposal from the Air Self-Defense Force last night, do you think it's still viable?"

"Prime Minister, I understand your feelings, but making a decision in the heat of the moment is not advisable."

"I'm just an ordinary man. I might have noble lineage but I'm just an ordinary man."

"No, Prime Minister. You're one of the few individuals qualified to occupy that seat when the nation faces a crisis. It's precisely because of your insight that you're capable of fulfilling that responsibility. The Chinese naval landing forces set out from the coast two hours ago. Taiwanese military bases are all but annihilated, but their fighters have landed at bases and civilian airports along the Ryukyu Islands."

"Does Taiwan have missiles that can target ships from land?"

"Yes, they do. But they've invested heavily in developing drones to counter ships. Although once they lose air superiority, the effectiveness of these drones may be significantly reduced. It'll be a tough fight."

"Understood. You may leave now."

"Should I convey a message to them?"

"Do you think it's necessary?"

"No. Expressing anger won't get through to that kind of opponent. Instead, maintaining a completely calm and collected demeanour is likely the only way our intent will get through."

"Then let's go with that. But tell them they have their work cut out for them…"

Katakura left the Executive Office at a quick pace. He hurried down the emergency stairs and jumped into the official car waiting at the curb, flanked by undercover police cars. The car headed out the back of the Prime Minister's Office and entered Sanno-zaka Rise, a road flanked by the Members of Office Building by the National Diet Building. Parked right there was a Mercedes Benz with diplomatic plates, squeezed between police cars. As Katakura approached, the driver of the Mercedes got out and opened the rear door. Katakura got inside. "Apologies for being late; I was talking to the prime minister."

"What'd he say?" asked Li Fudong, a minister from the Embassy of the People's Republic of China in Japan, in stern Japanese.

"About what?" Katakura feigned ignorance.

"About that...the mistarget. There's nothing more embarrassing than this."

"Ahh, that. Accidents happen."

"Look, I first want to personally express regret. It was an unacceptable launch that missed its target. Secondly, I apologise for the timing. Having studied Japanese diplomatic history, I can't help but recall the delay in notifying the U.S. government about the Pearl Harbor attack. But it seems Beijing intended to notify you after the attack."

"Was this an ultimatum?"

"That's the only way to take it, isn't it? But I envy you. Your country is a great civilization. Mine is barbaric. Since the NSA is likely intercepting and deciphering communications back home, I might as well speak frankly. Even though we've shown considerable generosity by not demanding unconditional surrender from Japan, there are those openly saying that there's no need to show any more courtesy than that."

"I don't remember much about the bubble era, but I heard that Japan was similarly arrogant back then. Buying up Hollywood studios and boasting about how the total value of land within the Yamanote Line could buy all the land in the U.S…"

"Japan's military cooperation with Taiwan, whatever form it may take, will not be tolerated. If Taiwanese military aircraft land at any Japanese airport, it will be considered aiding the enemy, and we will absolutely retaliate against those locations."

"Then I guess we have a problem. The airports on the islands along the Ryukyu chain are already overflowing with Taiwanese military aircraft, and as for the fighters that landed at Kadena, you'd have to take that up with the U.S. military. I wish you had at least informed us before you launched the missile."

"Yes, it was truly…tactless."

"Another mistarget would be troublesome. If civilians become victims, I'm not sure how long our patience will last."

"I will convey that home. I wish I could respond with some ironic comment, but such a terrible mistaken bombing should never have occurred. One day they'll say this was the decisive factor that brought Japan into the war. I'll negotiate with the homeland for compensation to be paid to the families of the victims. This will be a matter of honour for us Chinese."

"That would indeed be proper. Oh, and the prime minister had a message for you. He said to say you had your work cut out for you and you have his sympathy," Katakura said with a grin as he opened the car door and stepped out.

———

Live footage from a GSDF helicopter was being streamed into Air Defense Command Headquarters. Lieutenant General

Maruyama strolled into the Abyss Room, sat down on a chair, and watched the footage displayed on the monitor. The room, built without windows, was dim even during the day.

"I wonder if the prime minister would've approved our plan if we'd briefed it to him after this attack?" Colonel Habu commented.

"No, I don't think so," responded Maruyama. "I think he thought it was undignified for Japan to engage in such actions. I don't agree, but it's good to have that perspective."

"Glad I wasn't there. I would have grabbed him by the collar."

"But to think, using an HGV as a warning. We fired four Patriots and didn't even graze it…"

"When the electricity and television are restored, public opinion will boil over. It'll be unmanageable."

"The public will be horrified," Maruyama agreed, yet he worried that Japan might have missed its chance to enter the conflict. If the PLA secured a bridgehead in Taiwan, fighter jets alone wouldn't suffice. The situation might escalate to deploying ground troops for combat, which he doubted the public would desire, regardless of their outrage.

———

PLA Army First Lieutenant Kong felt what seemed to be a blast wave. The entire apartment vibrated as if it were struck by a wind, initially leading her to think it was an earthquake. But as the loud noises of helicopters and the sirens of fire trucks approached from all directions, she realised something was amiss.

Deciding they should investigate, Kong and her deputy, Sergeant Yan Cheng, under the Vietnamese alias Dang Quang Hao, went outside to take a look. The dust was terrible, and visibility was poor. They could smell burning. They set off and got as far as they could, seeing dozens of fire trucks lined up bumper-to-bumper. No barriers had been set up yet, but it was immediately clear that it was impossible to go forward because of the extensive debris.

"What do you think it was?"

"A gas explosion? A plane crash? The airport is closed, so it can't be a plane crash. A bomber couldn't fly this far, so it couldn't be that. That just leaves a missile attack. But why would they target a residential area?"

"We live so close to here."

"The ones that targeted this area wouldn't know that, though."

"This is unbelievable."

If they wanted to threaten the Japanese, there are surely other ways to do it, Kong thought. Why are we even here doing these sabotage activities? We're supposed to be conducting hybrid warfare with calculated psychological effects. This feels like we've suddenly started swinging a knife at a boxing match. Such a reckless strategy.

7

God of War

Senior Captain Lei Yan, 164th Marine Brigade operations officer aboard the 25,000-tonne Type 071 amphibious dock landing ship *Siming Shan* was roused from sleep in the officers' quarters. Once again, it was Commander Dai Yizhi, the brigade intelligence officer, who woke him up. Although they called the space 'officers' quarters', for these marines, it was just a temporary lodging until they landed.

"What are you, Commander Dai? My nanny or something?" Lei Yan remarked.

"As you say, sir, a senior captain should have the right to an aide-de-camp."

"I'd rather be alone. It's a bit weird having someone fussing on you all day."

"If only I could go up the ranks as quickly as you, sir."

"Tidy your hair and put on your boots."

The troops were already up. Lei Yan didn't know where they had come from, but he thought the military was harsh in the way it treated them. When Lei Yan appeared in the landing operation command and control room, he saw many unfamiliar people working there. They all turned to look at him. Their faces expressed concern wondering why the operations officer had showed up. "We at Taipei yet?" he asked to no one in particular.

"Are you still asleep, Lei?" said Senior Captain Wan Yangdong, the brigade's chief of staff, with a hint of admonishment.

"We'll be landing soon. I thought it was about time His Majesty The Emperor should wake up," said Rear Admiral Yao Yan, who always brought everyone together with his relaxed demeanour.

"We're a cruel military, sir. Not even granting shore leave to those marines who barely escaped with their lives," remarked Lei.

"That was to protect us from the risk of infection," replied the admiral.

"This all feels so strange though, sir. The PLA lost an entire battalion's worth of troops all up across both operations, so where did all these fresh troops come from? And why are we the core force ordered to charge in again after already suffering that terrible defeat? It's like they're trying to destroy evidence or something…having us go off and die."

"That's not the case at all, Lei. We captured Pratas Island successfully."

"Sir, we lost an entire company capturing that tiny speck of an island. And all those enemy forces we had surrounded ended up escaping!"

"You're right. I take it back. If I ever utter such nonsense again, correct me just the same. But among the military authorities, our Marine Brigade is touted as an ever-victorious military corps, and you're seen as a divinely inspired genius of military strategy."

"All lies."

"No doubt. But, with the conquest of Taiwan imminent, we can't exactly admit to the public that we tried to establish a bridgehead on Diaoyu Island only to be toyed with by an enemy one-tenth our size before fleeing home, can we? Their description of the 164th is just a means to boost morale. The 164th has been replenished by troops from other units and magically returned to its original size to participate in the invasion of Taiwan's main island. But I've also learned from you that honour is not to be sought after but something you stumble into. Since we don't know what dangers lie ahead, I've yielded the vanguard to others. We'll launch our landing in our own time only after the bridgehead is secured."

"Well then, I suppose I don't have any work to do, sir."

"For now, probably not. You just need to stay composed while admiring officers come asking to hear your war stories. Then boast smugly about how you fought dragons on Pratas Island and tamed tigers on Diaoyu Island. Easy, right? Although I'm sure, given your dislike of people, you'll find it annoying."

"Absolutely. Taiwan is waiting along the coast with a lineup of anti-ship missiles. Is there any chance of success…"

"Well, we have a plan, though whether it'll work is another matter. We'll find out soon enough. And even if we don't, it's not like we have a choice. We're out of options now. It's actually rather simple. Once the bridgehead is secured, we'll be able to move freely and there are plenty of places to hide. Even if someone gets injured, there are hospitals, and we have fellow countrymen all over the place."

"How optimistic are you about this, sir?"

"We should be optimistic if we can at least reflect on the lessons learnt from the fierce fighting over the Diaoyu Islands. But those who want the glory can have it. Our objective is the subjugation of Taiwan. Once we clear the way for landing forces to arrive, the tank units will be able to land. I don't think there will be much work to do. If we can hold out for just two days, we'll be able to hand over to the regular army units."

"That's great. Can I go back to sleep one more time? Just wake me up when we dock at a port somewhere…"

"But they all want to hear your analysis. God of War Lei Yan's commentary. They've come here expecting to be the very first to land on Taiwan's shores under your command. If that isn't possible, they at least want to observe the landing and listen to your analysis of its unfolding. That might be better than leading the charge into killing."

"This landing ship is so big; it's bound to be a target."

"But it sure is comfortable. It doesn't sway much, there are showers, and you can get coffee."

"Alright. Let's do it. It's better than landing as the vanguard."

Rear Admiral Yao reverently guided Lei Yan to the middle of the operations room. There was a diorama of Taiwan's main island, measuring about three metres on each side. Both seasoned and fresh officers were gathering around. The fresh officers clearly outnumbered the veterans, reflecting the sacrifices the unit had made recently. Their eyes gleamed with anticipation at hearing the live lecture from the *God of War*.

"Okay, team. So, the vanguard will deploy units in ninety minutes. The fleet's already in a position where the enemy can see our silhouettes from the coast. Air superiority is on our side, but it seems our air forces haven't yet pushed over Taiwan. The air defences on that island are like a hedgehog. Even if we drive away their fighters, it's still not safe."

An arrow sticker was placed pointing toward Taoyuan City, southwest of Taipei. This indicated that the main attack would target this location.

"Admiral, sir, were you involved in the invasion planning, asked Lei Yan?"

"No. I had my hands full in the Pratas Island operation. This plan was devised in Beijing. But it's reasonable."

"You mean attacking Taoyuan?" Lei Yan asked with a slightly mocking expression.

"To bring about a quick victory, we must aim for the enemy's throat."

"Taoyuan has the highest concentration of enemy infantry, artillery, and missiles on the island. The tiger's mouth. A huge trap. The Army is obsessed with a quick victory and is sure to aim for Taoyuan after landing. So apparently all we need to do is prepare a plan to crush them there."

"Fine, we get your point, but there's not anywhere else to land. To the north are only mountains; no sandy beaches suitable for a landing and no roads for movement. If we land south of Taoyuan and spend time capturing, say, Taichung City, the enemy won't surrender as long as Taipei remains entirely secure."

"Where exactly are we landing? Is it already decided?"

"No. If the enemy's attacks are intense, we can shift to another location. Otherwise, we'll land at the bridgehead secured by one of the other units. In other words, on Taoyuan's coastline, or a little further south around Hsinchu City."

"Sir, do you remember what happened on Pratas Island?"

"How could I forget? The enemy didn't interfere with our landing. We unloaded vehicles and supplies and were ready to advance, but he was nowhere to be seen. Next moment, a torrent of shells rained down on us. I get why the enemy did what he did there, but there's only one landing point on Pratas Island and it's the size of a putting green. Taoyuan, on the other hand, has a forty-kilometre-long flat coastline. It won't be easy for the enemy to narrow down targets there."

"Sir, the enemy has several divisions defending Taoyuan. He can shell us as much as he likes. Landing in Taoyuan is a fool's errand. It's suicidal."

"So, present us with your own plan."

"First, we abandon the idea of a short-term decisive battle. Why is everyone so fixated on that? There's only one reason. If it's reported that Taipei is on the brink of collapse, the world will sympathise, then Japan and the U.S. might intervene. So, it's become an absolute imperative to capture Taipei before that happens. That being the case, we should take a gradual approach that still prevents Japan and the U.S. from intervening. We land south of Taichung and secure a bridgehead. We subdue the surrounding cities but don't advance. We continue to provide supplies to the local population, not letting them prosper but also not letting them die, and simply encircle Taoyuan and Taipei. If we just leave them there for six months, the enemy's provisions will dry up. They'll starve and surrender. People won't die outright, but lack of resources won't make for dramatic television coverage, so it won't attract as much international attention. Once Taiwan realises that no one will help them, they'll eventually surrender under the weight of hunger. It's like waiting for a ripe persimmon to fall."

"Fine, but the Central Military Commission would never accept a plan like that. But how nice would it be if we were always given that kind of time buffer. Do you think our forces will land without resistance?"

"There will be some token resistance. But it's more efficient to crush landing forces after a landing."

"So, assuming our forces secure the bridgehead with minimal resistance, where do you think we should land?"

"Do you have the authority to choose, sir?"

"I do. Apparently I've earned that right. How about landing in Taichung City?"

"Before the reinforcements arrive? We'd be caught in a pincer attack from the north and south and completely wiped out. If it were up to me…" Lei Yan took up the pointer. Everyone leaned forward, waiting to see where he would point.

"The northern tip of the island, the Yangmingshan area."

There was an audible "Oh?" from all those looking on.

"Out of the question. That's a mountainous region. The roads are limited and narrow. Artillery fire from Taipei will rain down on us from long-range guns."

"Yes. And it's only twenty clicks to the centre of Taipei. They'll absolutely bombard us to no end. So, we don't bother with securing a bridgehead in the proper sense. To avoid artillery fire, we'll walk quickly inland. Run, even. It's just a straight twenty k walk to Taipei. How about that? We walk straight to the capital. By tomorrow morning, we'll have circumvented Yangmingshan and will be within striking distance of Taipei City."

Once again, the room murmured. Rear Admiral Yao now started to show a look of interest. "Hmm…What are your thoughts, CoS?"

"This is quite the dilemma," began Senior Captain Wan. "I've spent years researching landing sites, but I never considered anything this close to Taipei. If I'm understanding this right, the key to this plan is that we can use friendly forces as a diversion. The units that land first on Taoyuan's coastline will attract a significant portion of the enemy's attention. He'll likely assume that the next unit will land around Taichung City, aiming to geographically divide Taiwan. But if, all of a sudden, they receive intel that there's a unit landing at Yangmingshan, it could cause a panic. This might be worth considering."

"Senior Captain Lei, you really are a god of war," remarked Rear Admiral Yao. "Now, the roads are extremely narrow there — will that be okay?"

"Tanks won't really be an advantage here; not even for the units landing at Taoyuan City. And for us, vehicles will just be a hindrance when trying to break through mountainous areas, and Yangmingshan is a huge mountain. Getting lost won't be too big an issue. And there's plenty of water. If we're set on using roads, we'll have to break through before the enemy sets up a defensive line. It's like running a marathon. Keep the gear in vehicles and have the soldiers run lightly equipped. At the earliest, we'll be in Taipei by this evening, and the citizens will be in a panic. I'm not overly optimistic, though."

"Of course, defensive lines and positions will have already been established in some areas. But if the Taoyuan landing can at least be successful as an entry point, there's a chance that the enemy units positioned there will be drawn out. I don't think there'll be too thick a line of resistance remaining...CoS, thoughts?"

The chief of staff nodded twice, looking convinced.

"All right, then. After making a feint towards a Taoyuan landing, we'll manoeuvre and attempt a landing at Provincial Highway 2 here on the northern coastline. Company commanders, remain behind. We'll continue planning specific landing points for each company and the routes to move out from there."

With everyone still respectfully watching him, Senior Captain Lei put down his pointer and stepped back.

"As expected, Senior Captain Lei, sir, you're the real deal. You always come up with a divine plan right when we need it," praised Commander Dai.

"Enough of that. But what do you think? Do you think it'll work?"

"I don't want to land in Taoyuan only to play second fiddle to some other units, and I don't want to land in Taichung just to be surrounded. This is a terrifyingly sound plan. It's worth the risk."

"I need a coffee."

"Let's find some. Seems like you really do need an aide!"

In truth, this plan had been in the works since the moment they escaped from Diaoyu Island via the air-cushioned landing craft. It wasn't the best plan. At most, Lai thought it was better than getting wiped out elsewhere. There were countless obstacles. Of course, reaching Taipei in half a day wasn't going to happen, but if they could hole themselves up in the mountains, they could buy some time even if they were surrounded. During that time, they could count on friendly reinforcements. The main island of Taiwan was much closer to the Chinese mainland than Diaoyu Island. Plus, it was far from Japan, and that was important.

———

Lieutenant Colonel Liu Jianhong, commander of the Taiwan Air Force's 17th Squadron, took off from the crowded Kadena Air Base in an F-16V fighter jet and headed straight for Amami Oshima. Without any navigational aids, he managed to land on the Amami Airport runway on his first attempt. The facility, however, could hardly be considered an ideal military base.

Amami Airport was located at the northern tip of Amami Oshima. The runway and taxiway were built on part of a coral reef. The runway was two-thousand metres long, which served its purpose, but there was nothing else there except the runway. If a flying squadron was to deploy there, the only space where they could park the jets was the tiny area around the terminal building. Landing mats were laid beside the runway, and fighter jets were lined up there. The scene resembled an aircraft carrier.

As he taxied up to the front of the airport terminal building, a guide was there waiting for him. He parked at the edge and saw four F-15EX Eagle II fighter jets sitting there, loaded with

AMRAAM missiles. He couldn't believe that just four of these fighters could shoot down forty enemy planes.

When he got out of the cockpit, an Asian woman in a flight suit was waiting. However, she wasn't a member of the Japan Self-Defense Forces. She was a U.S. Air Force pilot who suddenly started speaking to him in Mandarin.

"I'm originally from Hong Kong, so I'm not that good with Mandarin. I hope you understand me," said Major Elsie Chan with a smile.

"Pardon?" replied Lieutenant Colonel Liu, bewildered. She explained that her family had fled Hong Kong years ago and settled in Hawaii, where she became an Air National Guard pilot and earned her instructor qualification for the EX. Liu was doubly astonished to hear that she was also one of those involved in shooting down those forty aircraft.

She spoke quickly while they walked. "Have you been able to contact Hualien Air Base?"

"No, we haven't. I don't even know if everyone's safe to be honest...or how many units managed to escape. We were at the U.S. base on Okinawa and we weren't able to communicate freely with other airfields."

"That's unfortunate. Most of the aircraft that escaped should be safe. The Aegis fleet shot down about 80 percent of the ballistic missiles aimed at the Ryukyu Islands."

"Are American pilots not flying the planes?"

"No, we're all back-seaters. Japanese pilots are flying. The controls aren't much different from the older Eagles, so everyone adapted quickly."

"We got the V model and flew after an abridged course. This feels, well, like a testing ground for new American weapons."

"Absolutely. Honestly, when you all rushed in without any prior coordination, the Japanese weren't too happy. But did you hear about the missile attack on Tokyo?"

"Yes. They showed me the aerial photos at Kadena. Just awful! Claiming they were targeting the riverbank is just a poor excuse. Beijing deliberately aimed for that residential area."

"Either way, what a strategic blunder! They probably wanted to scare the Japanese by deliberately firing a single missile, but surprisingly, the Japanese are tough. It seems they angered the Japanese government enough that they decided to respond more aggressively. That's why they've approved the EX unit deployed here in Amami, together with your V model squadron, to operate in the Taiwanese airspace to hold back the enemy."

"Did we get approval for ground attacks too? The EX is an updated Strike Eagle, which was originally a strike fighter."

"We'll have to figure that out later, but basically, we only came equipped for air-to-air, so for guided bombs and other munitions, we'd currently have to use Japan's inventory, and they're not fully compatible yet."

"Well, let's see if we can get air-to-ground munitions for the EXs procured from America asap. I'll contact the Taipei Representative Office in DC to pass on how urgent it is."

"That might be a good idea."

The command post had been set up inside the terminal building. They switched to English upon entering. Major Chan introduced Lieutenant Colonel Liu to Lieutenant Colonel Masaaki Hidaka, commander of the 307th Provisional Squadron, Lieutenant Colonel Oliver R. Evans, the operations officer of Kadena Air Base's 18th Wing and an instructor for the EX; and ASDF Captain Ai Shinjo, who flew with Major Chan.

"This is Captain Shinjo, callsign 'The Witch', who holds the kill score record for the ASDF. She achieved that count in just one mission."

"Oh, all I did was pull the trigger — or press the switch rather," Shinjo said humbly.

Black-and-white photos were pinned to the whiteboard. "These just arrived from Tokyo," Hidaka explained. They were the latest images of Hualien Air Force Base. "As you can see, the ballistic missile attack caused significant damage. The hangars are completely destroyed. The command building remains standing but appears heavily damaged from the blast. However, they managed to block much of the follow-on cruise missile saturation attack. The neighbouring cave hangar should be somewhere around here…" Hidaka pointed.

Liu corrected him, indicating with his finger. "It's here…and it seems to be intact. I don't see any signs of penetration bombs."

"That's good. It looks like the underground fuel tanks are safe, and the runway damage is repairable, though it'll take time."

"Yes. It looks like we can still rebuild." The Taiwanese lieutenant colonel sighed in relief.

"Now, to discuss the specifics…" began Lieutenant Colonel Evans. "It seems you haven't lost air superiority yet. The Chinese aircraft aren't approaching your main island, probably intimidated by your SAMs."

"That's good news. But the enemy will surely push sooner or later," said Liu.

"Indeed," continued Evans. "Unfortunately, enemy landing forces will soon be all over Taoyuan's coastline. PLA aircraft will be providing support overhead at the same time. We'll sortie to target them. From here in Amami, it's about a thousand clicks to Taiwan's west coast if we fly directly. To avoid Chinese coastal radar, we should fly east of Okinawa Island and then attack from the east. This will mean flying over twelve-hundred kilometres one way. This is a joint operation between Japan, the U.S., and Taiwan. Japan will contribute the EXs and pilots. We'll provide aircrew and tankers. The Taiwanese military will contribute F-16V fighters and E-2K early-warning aircraft to support the operation. The JASDF will control the entire mission from the E-767 AWACS. I apologise for making this decision without consulting you first, Colonel Liu, but…"

"Not a problem at all! If I may make one request, could you allow me to join the AWACS crew as a controller? It might be useful."

"You'll have to figure out a way to get onto it mid-air," Evans said this with a straight face, causing Liu to look bewildered for a moment.

"Oh, stop that, Colonel Evans!" interjected Major Chan. She turned to Lieutenant Colonel Liu and spoke in Mandarin. "Sorry about that, sir. The AWACS is already airborne. Americans tend to make jokes even in times like these…"

"Naha is currently repairing its runway. I'll check if the AWACS can temporarily land at Kadena," Shinjo added.

"Thank you very much. I'll head back to Kadena immediately to finalise the mission with the squadron and the E-2K aircrew."

"Please do that. This will be an ongoing mission. We'll sortie multiple times a day to irritate the PLA and make it clear we're not giving up air superiority. Ultimately, the enemy troops that land will end up isolated."

"This is an excellent plan. Exactly what we've been waiting for! This will boost the morale of the troops back home." Lieutenant Colonel Liu, dashed out of the terminal building, barely able to contain his excitement. Major Chan chased after him.

"Sir! Regarding the evacuated aircraft…You know there are over a hundred Taiwanese IDF fighters crammed in at Shimoji Island Airport. I don't think that's going to work. They can only use what they have on board for maintenance, and their capability leaves a bit to be desired."

"Understood. Do you think the USAF would accept them at Andersen in Guam?"

"That's above my paygrade, sir. But I've been thinking. The IDF fighters are still somewhat usable. And the JASDF can't neglect its northern defence role. North Korea still needs to be monitored, although I don't expect much to happen there. Meanwhile, the JASDF's F-15Js are practically antiques, probably on par with your IDFs. So, how about having Taiwan's IDF fighters take on Japan's air alert duties in the north, allowing the JASDF to move its more capable aircraft south? This way, we can maintain strong defences in the north and better employ our modern aircraft in the south. Just something I've been thinking about."

"That could work. I'll raise it up the chain. Although at the moment I have no idea what the chain-of-command even looks like. Hopefully someone from Air Force Command managed to escape."

"Thank you. I'll also gently raise it with the Japanese side. Hong Kong once shone brilliantly in Asia, but she's been dirtied like an old rag. Beijing must be punished."

"By all means, let's do it!"

Lieutenant Colonel Liu started the engine, lit the afterburners, and took off. He hoped that with the V models and EXs working together, a single force package could scatter the swarming Chinese.

———

Colonel Hikaru Shiba checked each piece of equipment laid out on the table in the hidden room behind the hotel's ballroom. The small, elderly man with sunglasses standing in front of her had the peculiar habit of speaking in an unusually low voice, and his expression never changed. He read off the items one by one.

"Chest rig…check, hydration pack…check, Maglite… check, FAST helmet with night vision goggles…check. Tactical vest and plate carrier…check. I hope this bayonet is to your liking…Dagger, tactical ankle knife, knee pads, all check. All camouflage colours have been chosen to blend into Taiwan's mountainous terrain this season."

"What should we do if it turns into urban guerrilla warfare? What about IR lights for the FAST helmets?"

"Sorry, we're all out, and they're not something we usually carry. But I'll try and have them delivered to the front desk by evening. As for firearms, we've got an HK416 with a suppressor and six magazines. There are also two pistols. I hope these suit your needs as well…"

"The barrel is new, right?" Colonel Shiba asked, peering into the muzzle of the assault rifle.

"Our credibility is paramount, Madam Colonel."

"Yes. I see."

"And also, the requested Starlink satellite phone."

"Right. Overall, pretty good. Pushing stuff like this through the black market must give the police a hard time."

"Of course, we don't sell to just anyone."

"How much is it all," asked Wang Wenxiong. "I can deposit a hundred thousand USD worth of Bitcoin into that account."

"Absolutely not!" The old man showed emotion on his face for the first time. "Your father gave us strict orders. If the enemy attacks, we are to provide maximum cooperation."

"I see. And how is that other matter progressing?"

"If it comes to that, it will be a terrifying situation, but my sons are doing the rounds. It would be an honour if you were to lead them, Madam Colonel."

"Understood. That's all for now — I'll count on you if anything else comes up."

The old man gave a slight bow to the customers in the corner of the room and then left.

Shiba gripped the bayonet in her right hand, which she had taken from its holster, and muttered, "It'll take some time to get used to this…"

Retired Vice Admiral Wang Zhihou, former commander of the Taiwanese Marine Corps, laughed and commented, "Unbelievable! Never mind the pistols, but how are assault rifles circulating? And they look almost brand new."

"My father planned to put me on a smuggling boat to join guerrilla activities if the PLA attacked," said Shiba. "He was adamant about it."

"Do you think it will come to that?" asked Wang Wenxiong, a.k.a. Fumio. He and Admiral Wang were related.

"I pray it won't," said Shiba. "As a JSDF liaison officer, the last thing I want is to be running around the mountains with people from the Taiwanese Presidential Office. But if it comes to that, we'll need all the equipment we can get. On another topic, you need to do something about Xiaochao. It's too dangerous for her to stay in Taipei, and she'd only be a burden."

"She's just like you, Miss Shiba. Better give up on that idea."

"So, Admiral, are you up to something again with that 'red book' of yours?"

"That was the plan. I was trying to come up with some ideas to get Japan to fully join the war. But since those idiots decided to fire a ballistic missile into Tokyo, I've decided there's no need anymore. I just don't get it. Organisations make such fatal errors of judgement sometimes. Why they thought intimidating the Japanese with that kind of threat would silence them is beyond me…"

"Of course, it's all for the sake of a market of 1.4 billion." Shiba, wearing a GSDF service dress skirt, wrapped a tactical knife holster around her left ankle, placed the folded small knife into it, and hid it with her white sock.

"I'm guessing you won't be able to hide a pistol in your socks like that?"

"When I change into combat uniform I'll fit it over my tac boots. So what's the situation in Taoyuan?"

"NSTR. Once they land and begin their advance, the shelling will start. What a mess. They're coming all this way just to be annihilated. Just between us, this war is already decided. The enemy is so afraid of our SAMs that he won't send a single attack helicopter or fighter jet. We're making out like we'll be surrendering Taipei by tomorrow just to get some help, but in reality, Beijing is losing badly in this war. Right?" The admiral turned to Fumio.

"I'm not sure about that, Uncle. You're a bit overconfident."

"Is that so? Taoyuan may be the only landing spot, but it's not a place you'd normally want to attack from."

"So where would you land?"

"Taoyuan, of course. It's the only viable landing spot. Taichung is too far from Taipei."

"The enemy fully understands the difficulties of the mission."

"That's right. But I'd like to propose a landing site for the Japanese Amphib Brigade. What do you think?"

"There's only Keelung and Yilan, isn't there? You're not suggesting they go around to the Taiwan Strait side to land, are you?"

"We could strike the landed enemy from behind."

"If Domon heard that, he'd jump to the rafters in excitement," commented Shiba.

"In any case, the suffering of the citizens of Taipei will be brief. The enemy will regret the whole damn thing."

Shiba packed the equipment on the table into a camouflage bag. She hoped she wouldn't have to use it, but the thought of returning home without using it somehow didn't sit right with her.

———

Commander Song Qin, leader of the PLA's Jiaolong Assault Team, landed at Niigata Airport in a fresh suit and plain black tie. He was posing as Oleg Penkovsky, Second Secretary at the Russian Ministry of Foreign Affairs.

The Russian Embassy had even sent a staff member from Tokyo to pick him up. It was an official car, a black-painted Prius proudly displaying the Russian flag. He had no idea where the group from the GSDF Amphibious Brigade went after leaving the airport, but he did know that the Prius he was in was being tailed.

Ivan Tsurenko, Second Secretary from the Embassy came to pick him up, seemed unbothered. He spoke Japanese with better pronunciation than Song Qin. This was his second assignment in Japan, and he had already been living there for seven years. Song Qin felt envious. "Do you get tailed every day?"

"Of course! Round the clock. The Russian embassy and the Tokyo Metropolitan Police Department's Public Security Bureau are very close comrades! We spend more time together than with our families. You'll leave the embassy in the evening in a delivery van. Don't use trash bins. The police collect everything and inspect it; they'll open every last tissue. They do the same to the Chinese embassy."

The car continued on the lower roads. The highways were closed because it was difficult to deal with accidents if they occurred there. It wasn't too congested. Tsurenko explained that the roads heading out of Tokyo were somewhat busy, but the roads heading into Tokyo were probably less congested than usual.

To Song Qin everything was new and interesting. The roadside signs, in particular, were fascinating. If he had been alone, he probably would have read each one out loud. "You Russians are a kind people," he said to Tsurenko.

"Oh, there's a reason for this. The Chinese embassy in Berlin did us a favour the month before last. I don't know any of the details. This is apparently a token of appreciation for that. We have orders from Moscow to carry this out perfectly. But you Chinese need to study hybrid warfare a bit more. That was reckless…firing a missile into a residential area…"

"I think it might have been an accident."

"Do you believe that? I don't. Even if it was an accident, if Russia accidentally fired a missile into Fifth Avenue in New York, it would lead to war. Saying one of your missiles misfired…C'mon! Not a chance."

"Sure…" Song Qin couldn't understand what the Joint Staff Department was thinking. If they were going to do something like that, maybe target Nagoya or Osaka. But targeting the heart of the capital was shocking. "But don't you think the blackout and internet shutdown have been effective?"

"It was a huge inconvenience! I couldn't use the internet, and last night, with nothing to do, I went to bed at eight. My wife didn't want to spend time with me. I had no outlet for my… erm…pent-up desires. It was miserable."

"My apologies on behalf of the Chinese government." It couldn't have been a mistake, Song thought. Then he remembered that a female student he studied with over Zoom lived in the Setagaya area. He hoped she was safe.

———

Minami Komachi cleaned inside and outside the store before waking the convenience store proprietress. The dust was terrible. The neighbourhood was still in turmoil. Helicopters appeared one after another, flying low and circling overhead. She thought they were a nuisance, especially since there were no TV broadcasts being aired anymore. Meanwhile, faxes kept pouring in. Some included official statements from the Government of Japan and Tokyo Metropolitan Government regarding the incident. She made large copies of them and posted them outside the store.

Minami finally woke up the proprietress who had slept for over twelve hours straight, the blast not even waking her. Minami gave her some water to drink and, while clearing the cardboard laid out in the office, reported on what had happened in the past twelve hours.

The proprietress immediately went and checked the addresses of the twenty part-time workers who worked there. Fortunately, it seemed none of them lived in the vicinity of the affected area. Even in Setagaya, it was not uncommon for the wives of upper-class residents, who owned houses in the area, to work part-time at convenience stores as a way of passing the time. "It must have been frightening! Especially for Yasu, we need to thank him! Do you think he'll come back here after helping at the other store?"

"Probably not. He seemed exhausted."

"Minami, you can go home for today. Don't worry about your shift tonight."

"No. Ma'am, you should go home and take a shower — oh, I guess there's no hot water. Please change your clothes. I can handle things for another hour or two."

"Please go. It's not like I'm heading out for tea at Futako Tamagawa. I'm fine in these clothes. Really, you should go home and rest."

"If you insist...But please look through the faxes. I've stacked them in the order they arrived. I've also made a list of the people we hired temporarily since yesterday. They all worked very hard. They truly put their hearts into it. I have a new appreciation for the residents of this area."

"Oh, good. The wealthy can be kind as long as their interests aren't affected."

Minami took off her jacket and finally headed home. It had been a long night. At the rental bicycle space, she noticed that three bicycles had been returned. They didn't seem to be the ones rented from here, but she was impressed by the people's conscientiousness even in times like these.

8

Climb Mount Niitaka!

Members of the 164th Marine Brigade sat facing the large screen in the landing operations command and control room aboard the 25,000-tonne Type 071 amphibious dock landing ship *Siming Shan*. The operation about to commence, if successful, would be widely proclaimed as the most brilliant achievement of the People's Liberation Army and would fulfil the greatest aspiration of the People's Republic of China since its establishment.

Ahead of them, the East Sea Fleet and South Sea Fleet were arrayed along a line twenty kilometres from the coast of Taiwan, spanning fifty kilometres north to south. A total of thirty landing ships had been readied. If they succeeded in landing on the coastline of Taoyuan, securing a bridgehead and advancing forward, the ferry units would promptly advance and enter Hsinchu Port south of Taoyuan to disembark ground forces and capture Hsinchu Air Base. The landing forces then planned to head north to seize Taoyuan International Airport and deploy aviation forces to the north and south of Taoyuan.

The fleet sat line abreast and the order to advance was issued. Small vessels emerged, weaving through the large ships and kicking up white wakes. There were over twenty of them. From a distance, they looked like nothing more than pleasure craft. A drone sending aerial footage zoomed in on one of the small vessels. A prominent satellite communication dome was mounted at the rear of the hull. The entire hull was painted white. While there appeared to be a bridge section, square radar arrays were fitted where one would expect windows. A cannon was also mounted on the bow.

Senior Captain Wan Yangdong, the Brigade's chief of staff, commenced his brief over the microphone. "This is the pride of our navy, the smallest yet most powerful unmanned Chinese aegis ship. The West has named it the 'Mini-Aegis'. It's fifteen metres long and displaces only twenty tonnes. The prototype carried unnecessary items like torpedoes, but these ones are equipped with four small anti-aircraft missiles mounted in vertical launch systems and four more in horizontal launch systems on both sides. The missiles are also capable of anti-tank attacks. Its main gun is a thirty-millimetre rapid-fire cannon. These ships are operating line abreast, spaced so that their cannons can cover each other."

The screen switched, showing the full-length flight deck of the Type 075 amphibious assault ship. Medium-sized drones began launching one after another from rails equipped with auxiliary rocket propulsion devices. Attack helicopters also took off.

Hand launched kamikaze drones took off from the rear flight deck of the Type 071 amphibious dock landing ship. These drones, carrying one one-kilogram bombs, locked onto the sources of enemy anti-air missile radar waves, diving in for the attack.

The unmanned 'Mini-Aegis' ships accelerated and charged towards the coastline. It was a spectacular sight. There were no opponents to resist them, and no sign that the unmanned fleet would be stopped. Destroying even one of these unmanned ships was highly inefficient. Missiles fired at them would be intercepted by anti-aircraft missiles or the thirty-millimetre cannon. To sink a single ship, it would likely take four to five anti-ship missiles targeting simultaneously.

When the unmanned fleet reached ten kilometres offshore, Type 05 amphibious fighting vehicles and armoured personnel carriers launched from the landing ships.

As the Mini-Aegis fleet approached five kilometres offshore, they slowed down to wait for the forces behind them. When the Type 05 amphibious fighting vehicles caught up, the main force of the air-cushioned landing craft commenced their advancement. There were fifteen of them.

Rear Admiral Yao Yan sighed. "Had we been given even half of these for the Diaoyu mission, we could have landed an entire battalion at once…"

The drone forces crossed the coastline and began their reconnaissance mission, searching for prey. But there was nothing moving on land. There was no sign of the enemy, nor were there any foxholes. The tranquil rural area seemed completely deserted, the drones occasionally detecting only the odd stray dog.

The timing of the air-cushioned landing craft and the Type 05 amphibious fighting vehicles was coordinated to ensure simultaneous landing. Just before that, the surface fleet began providing covering fire. Smoke shells were launched simultaneously at the coastline. Drones carrying mortar-type shells dropped smoke bombs at designated targets.

The two-hundred-kilometre-long coastline was covered in patchwork shrouds of smoke, obscuring visibility. The wind blew from the sea, causing the smoke to blind the Taiwanese forces dug in on the land.

The air-cushioned landing craft made their landing amidst all this. They were programmed to launch red flares the moment they beached and opened their front decks. Red flares rose one after another at roughly five-hundred metre intervals from the ones that successfully landed. Infantry disembarked and dispersed, followed by tanks and armoured vehicles. Overhead, a force of Ka-52K attack helicopters purchased from Russia provided cover.

"Now this is what you call a flawless landing operation. It looks like something out of a training video," the chief of staff said bitterly, recalling their previous blunders.

Less than two minutes later, having landed the troops and vehicles, the air-cushioned landing craft immediately withdrew from the coastline to bring in the next wave of forces. No missiles, shells, or bullets had yet been fired.

Rear Admiral Yao stood in front of the screen, looked at his subordinates, and took the microphone. "Well, marines, things certainly are looking bright. This is a significant victory and achievement for our People's Liberation Army. Now let's carry out our mission. After the second friendly force wave launches, our formation will change course and head towards our own landing site. You will board the air-cushioned landing craft and landing boats and take command of your units...Why those gloomy faces? Did you want our forces to be crushed? We'll land at a location closer to Taipei than the other formations. There will be opportunities to make up for it. Now heads up and advance!"

Senior Captain Lei Yan remained silent. His expression revealed nothing about the upcoming developments.

Around twenty-thousand troops, organised into three brigades, were on the Taoyuan coastline within an hour. Behind them, the helicopter assault forces awaited the signal to launch. No one doubted the success of the mission. They believed the

Taiwanese military had lost the will to fight, terrified by the massive fleet, mobility, and large troop numbers.

Even Rear Admiral Yao wondered if it might be safer to land as part of the third wave. He speculated that the Taiwanese military's communication networks had been disrupted, preventing the transmission of orders. He felt certain that their victory was due to their earlier achievement of network modernisation and efficient organisation of drone units. Nevertheless, with some trepidation, he ordered his formation to change course.

He wondered if Vice Admiral Tang Dongming, who commanded the East Sea Fleet from the second forty-thousand tonne Type 075 amphibious assault ship *Huashan*, was starting to regret accepting the proposal. "This is Lei Yan's plan!" Yao had declared. "I trust his judgement," Vice Admiral Tang had responded without any hesitation.

————

By the time the second wave of landing forces reached the beach, the Japan-Taiwan fighter formations were marshalling south of Ishigaki Island. Twelve ASDF F-15EX fighters were flying in groups of four, orbiting at a low altitude below the reach of Chinese radar, two-hundred kilometres off the coast of Hualien.

The Taiwanese Air Force's F-16V fighter squadron's launch, however, had been delayed, caused by the time taken for the pre-mission briefing. There was also debate whether to arm with bombs or air-to-air munitions. Given the landing had already commenced, and since the EX fighters could handle the control of the air mission, they wanted to support the friendly ground forces with bombs. But they weren't carrying guided bombs or air-to-ground missiles. Borrowing Mk-82 bombs from the U.S. military was an option, but ultimately, they took off with an air-to-air loadout because they couldn't guarantee coordination with ground forces.

Taiwanese Air Force Lieutenant Colonel Liu Jianhong, Commander of the 17th Squadron, was able to board the ASDF AWACS after all. Although it was frustrating not to be able to take hold of a HOTAS and lead the formation, his subordinates would pull the trigger on the missiles. But when it came to controlling the formation, there was no one else but him.

Through satellite communications, they received constant updates on the movements of the PLA. The information came from U.S. reconnaissance satellites and probably stealth drones. Still, they had to endure for now. They had no choice but to wait until the enemy fighters appeared.

The signal for the counterattack came from the Ministry of National Defense in Taipei. In the underground military command centre of the Ministry of National Defense building across the Keelung River from the old Songshan Airfield, Defence Minister Gu Jinqiang had donned his Marine Corps combat uniform for the first time in a long time and sat at the head of the table, sleeplessly preparing for that moment. A rear admiral stood behind Gu and whispered something in his ear.

"I see, the third wave has shifted. That was Yao Yan's landing force, wasn't it? They probably noticed how quiet it all was. Well, my friends, I propose that we signal the counterattack. What do you think?"

All the star ranks surrounding the table nodded in agreement. Gu Jinqiang placed his hands on the table, leaned forward, and stood up. Then, he spoke again, this time with a commanding voice.

"To all forces! To all forces! Climb Mount Niitaka! Commence the counterattack!"

All at once, telephones were picked up, and the command 'Climb Mount Niitaka!' echoed throughout the room.

On the western coast of Taoyuan City, a Thunderbolt multiple rocket launcher, hidden in the Dongyanshan National Forest Recreation Area thirty kilometres inland from the coastline, fired twelve rockets. None of them, however, was intended for ground attack. The rockets ascended and exploded one after another approximately three hundred metres above the coastline, spreading seven-colour smoke over the enemy forces. This was the signal to commence the counterattack if they were under enemy jamming.

Multiple rocket launchers, long-range artillery, and mortar units arrayed along the coastline began firing simultaneously over a span of twenty kilometres north to south. They didn't move positions, but continued firing relentlessly until they exhausted their ammunition. Within a mere minute, the coastline was engulfed in darkness.

There was no way the PLA forces could counterattack; the thick smoke rendered even outstretched hands invisible. Naval gunfire had destroyed the obstacles on the coastline, leaving the soldiers with no escape. All they could do was lie prone and crawl under the newly landed tanks and armoured vehicles or seek refuge in ditches.

The bombardment continued for nearly ten minutes, altering the terrain of the coastline. Newly offloaded munitions exploded, further destroying surrounding vehicles and soldiers. The PLA's attack helicopter force, which had been loitering offshore, began to advance, but the intense smoke prevented them from getting close. They could only fire rockets towards the town, and they made sure not to approach within five kilometres of the coastline to avoid being attacked.

It took more than ten minutes for the sea breeze to clear the smoke. Once the smoke cleared, there was no movement; only calls for medics and inhuman screams. A single Type 99A tank, having endured the bombardment, began to move forward, swinging its turret left and right. But before it advanced twenty metres, an anti-tank missile came from nowhere. Then a second, then a third missile hit, causing the tank to explode spectacularly and fall silent.

After the smoke cleared, the tank hunt began. Infantry units hidden in residential areas and fields began a simultaneous launch of anti-tank missiles at the tanks. The repeated bombardments had damaged the enemy vehicles' optical sensors, preventing them from noticing the incoming missiles, leaving them immobilised.

Thirty minutes after the Taiwanese counterattack began, fighter and attack aircraft from the Chinese mainland coast finally pushed. They were under the assumption that there were no enemy fighters. At that time, Colonel Hao Fei's KJ-600 early warning aircraft was flying at an altitude of 10,000 feet along the mainland coast. This altitude was sufficient to monitor the Taoyuan coastline, but it was too far and too low to detect enemy formations hiding at low altitude beyond the Taiwanese Central Mountain Range. On her scope, Hao could clearly see the Taiwanese Air Force's E-2K and Japan's AWACS operating over the Pacific Ocean, along with the fighters patrolling to protect them, but she was completely unaware of the enemy formations hiding below the mountains.

The Taiwanese Air Force's F-16Vs were the first to ascend and briefly showed themselves over Taoyuan. They launched AMRAAM missiles at the attack helicopters loitering offshore. For the AMRAAMs, the helicopters were sluggish, and their radar cross sections large. The attack helicopters attempted evasive manoeuvres and dispensed chaff and flares, but they fell one by one, disintegrating and crashing into the sea.

From the ASDF AWACS, Lieutenant Colonel Liu Jianhong quickly instructed the F-16V formation back down below the mountains before they could become targets for the Chinese Mini-Aegis ships offshore. Their goal was not to eliminate the attack helicopter forces but to act as bait, luring the enemy fighters to the eastern side of the mountain range.

Mixed groups of J-10 and J-11 fighters, eager to avenge the helicopters, lit their afterburners and charged in. Colonel Hao Fei knew right away what was about to happen. It was the enemy's usual tactic. "What are they doing diving into the shadow of the mountain range!" she screamed in frustration.

She climbed to a higher altitude and moved towards Taiwan, directing all fighter aircraft to turn back. Most of the J-10s, with their inferior acceleration, managed to turn back just in time, but the J-11 pilots, with their powerful aircraft and matching egos, pushed in regardless.

———

Flying at a thousand feet along Taiwan's eastern coast, Captain Shinjo's four-ship formation of F-15EXs operated under radio silence. They emitted no signals, including from their powerful AESA radars, but they were receiving real-time updates on enemy movements from the AWACS.

Once again, like two days ago, they would use the infrared search and track system in their Legion Pods to enable the launch of their AMRAAMs. Formations of twenty enemy fighters appeared over the mountains. As they pursued the F-16V fighters fleeing towards the Pacific, the F-15EXs' AMRAAM missiles dove from high above, striking the enemy fighters before they even realised. One after another, the enemy fighters were shot down before they could reach the Pacific Ocean.

"You keep making the same stupid mistakes," Shinjo spat inside her mask. They obviously hadn't shared their combat experiences from two days prior.

Seizing the opportunity, a four-ship formation of Taiwanese Air Force P-3C patrol aircraft armed with Harpoon anti-ship cruise missiles crossed the mountains. Each launched four missiles in sea-skimming mode towards a pre-designated area without designating targets. The Harpoons hit two landing ships and two air-cushioned landing craft that couldn't evade in time. Chinese Mini-Aegis ships managed to shoot down the remaining missiles. PLA Navy warships out on the horizon gave up on supporting their ground forces and began to gradually retreat towards the mainland coast.

———

The Taiwan Marine Corps' 'Iron Force' 99th Brigade was positioned in reserve at the mountainous Yangmingshan National Park just north of Taipei. With an elevation of only eleven-hundred metres, it wasn't a high mountain, but its proximity to Taipei and hot springs made it a popular area with Japanese tourists. It was also well known for its scenic hiking trails.

This fight was primarily one for the Army, with the Marine Corps set to play a role in cutting down the enemy when he was cornered.

The Iron Force had already fought valiantly as the fighting unit on Pratas Island. For them, this was almost like a vacation. If the enemy were to land, they would naturally want to be the first to rush to the battlefield, but it was also important to let the Army have their turn.

Colonel Chen Zhiwei, who commanded the unit, did not feel rushed. He intended to sit back for a while and watch how the Army fought. Had he had the time, he would have relaxed in a hot spring. They had, in fact, entered the mountains in a leisurely manner, as if on a hike, and took their positions.

The battlefield was forty kilometres away. They couldn't see much. At best, by climbing a high point and using large binoculars, they could just make out the silhouettes of PLA Navy warships on the distant horizon.

They received no radio communication about the enemy landing and had no idea what was happening, but they did receive the message signalling the start of the counterattack: Climb Mount Niitaka. They were surprised that the sound of the bombardment reached them from so far away. It was an incredible sound, like thunder in the summer.

"I don't get it...They just got smashed using the same tactics at Pratas Island, and yet they were still dawdling on the coastline? Are they so stupid that they can't even learn from experience?"

"It's hard to forget doctrine drilled into you in the classroom," said Operations Officer Lieutenant Colonel Huang Junnan, standing on the scenic mountainside.

It felt strange to Chen that they were there idly watching the enemy from this picturesque place. But both he and Lieutenant Colonel Huang had withstood three days and nights, surrounded by an overwhelming enemy force on Pratas Island, before successfully evacuating the unit by submarine. The success of the evacuation mission, named Operation Kiska, greatly encouraged the people of Taiwan.

"The enemy won't come back again after this? Maybe this is the end? After all those grandiose claims, their landing force has been annihilated. The President will have to resign in disgrace. Shall we go to a hot spring? No one will mind. We didn't even get a break after returning."

"Indeed. We don't get the chance to come here often, so why not take a dip in the hot spring before we head down the mountain…"

Thirty metres behind them, a radio operator was muttering something. "Message not heard! Speak slower!"

"What's going on? Keep your voice down, you're spoiling the tranquillity."

"Yes, sir. I apologise. It's from the western frontline outpost. Dragon seems to be reporting something, but the jamming makes it hard to hear clearly…" intelligence officer Major Wu Jinfeng reported apologetically.

"Dragon? That's Sergeant Liu Jinlong, right? He'd only be using the radio outside of scheduled communications in an emergency…"

"Well, I'm not sure. Maybe there was an accident on one of the hiking trails?"

"Someone, send a fast runner."

"I'll try again. Sometimes the signal improves."

A clearer signal finally came through and the radio operator listened and took notes. Colonel Chen noticed that his fingers had started to tremble.

"A formation offshore! An amphibious formation has appeared offshore!"

"Isn't that the enemy fleet returning to home port?"

"No, the bows are pointed this way, the bows are pointed this way. The air-cushioned landing craft are coming out!"

"What? That's impossible. Who would be foolish enough to land here? There's no proper beach, and the roads are so narrow that tanks can't even pass... Oh, shit…" The colonel realised and cursed. "It's Rear Admiral Yao Yan's force! That genius strategist Lei Yan is doing it again. So, they used their own troops as bait, knowing they'd be annihilated?"

"Let's request artillery support. If we intercept them at the coastline…" suggested Lieutenant Colonel Huang.

"No good. Lei Yan won't waste time leisurely stacking ammo boxes on the beach to create a bridgehead. He'll cross Provincial Highway 2 and climb the mountain! It's only twenty clicks to Taipei. They plan to invade Taipei before nightfall. Launch the red flares! Order all units to prepare for combat. Yao Yan and Lei Yan, those two who cornered us on Pratas Island, are coming again!"

"It seems we have quite an affiliation with them."

"Yes, but this time, it's our turn to welcome them. We won't let them leave empty-handed. Let's reconsider the location of our command post. We mustn't let them break through the line of defence!"

Red flares soared into the sky. The sun was already setting, but once the line was breached, there were no forces left to stop them before they reached Taipei. They had to hold the line here at all costs.

Epilogue

Minami Komachi did not wake up until it was dark because of the fatigue she had accumulated. Despite the proprietress insisting that she skip her next shift, Minami still felt a sense of duty to go. By the second day, there had been a faint hope that the electricity might be restored, but that hope was soon thoroughly dashed. The electricity and mobile phone networks were still out. Minami didn't have a radio, but she figured there wouldn't be any broadcasts anyway.

Even now, groups of high school students with megaphones were still marching through the streets. The situation had not improved at all since yesterday. Minami got ready while holding the Mini Maglite in her mouth. She gave up on putting on makeup, thinking it didn't matter. Her hair, too, didn't need to impress anyone.

She decided to go out by bicycle again today. The LED light on the bicycle was brighter than the Mini Maglite. After she started pedalling her bicycle, she suddenly decided to change her route. Setagaya was mostly flat, but there were a few little wooded hills. Thinking she might be able to see Tokyo Tower, she headed towards Shibuya.

Several families with flashlights were walking in the same direction. This was probably the right way. She soon reached a slope and got off her bicycle to push it. There was a small cut-through, and directly above it was a small open space that looked like a park. It was crowded with people. After climbing up the cut-through, she followed the crowd and approached the park. The park was filled with people as if a concert was taking place and it seemed impossible to enter. The lights of Tokyo Tower would be on for fifteen minutes. Just a glimpse of it would be enough. She wasn't here with a boyfriend, after all.

As it got closer to eight o'clock, the children started counting down. The adults joined in for the last ten seconds. The moment Tokyo Tower's lights came back on, there was a great round of applause and cheers. But it wasn't what she had expected. It looked like the tip of a pen peeking over the rooftops of the houses. Even so, it was definitely Tokyo Tower. She thought about her mother and father and wondered if they had ever seen Tokyo Tower.

I'm sorry, everyone, she thought. I had completely forgotten you all until today. I had sealed away everything that happened that day. What happened to you, what happened to me, and what happened to our hometown, all those memories I locked away.

She couldn't help it. Forgetting was the only way she could survive. She couldn't even remember her mother's, father's, sister's or brother's birthdays. The only date she could remember, the one she couldn't forget even if she tried, was 3.11, the anniversary of their deaths. Even today, she struggled in the darkness...she struggled, but lived on, dreaming of something better tomorrow.

Minami wiped away her tears.

That night, many Japanese people shed tears upon witnessing the night view of Tokyo Tower. But the tears Minami shed were for a different reason.

Continued in Part Two.

ABOUT THE AUTHOR

Eiji Oishi is a Japanese author known for his techno-thrillers and military suspense novels. He made his literary debut in 1986 with Pursue the B-1 Bomber and has since gone on to write hundreds more Oishi's books have garnered a dedicated following, and several titles have become bestsellers.

Oishi's writing is often compared to that of Tom Clancy, with intricate plots and detailed military technology. His ability to blend speculative fiction with real-world geopolitical scenarios has made his works popular among fans of military fiction.

The fictional Japanese Self-Defense Forces special operations unit 'The Silent Corps' features regularly in his works.

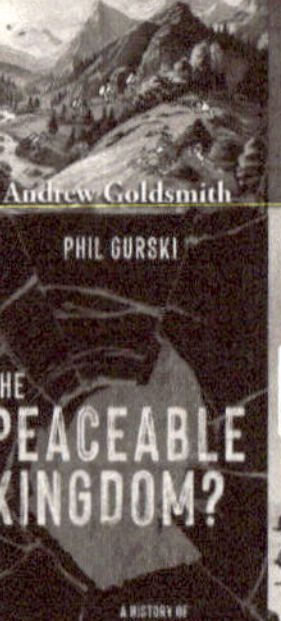

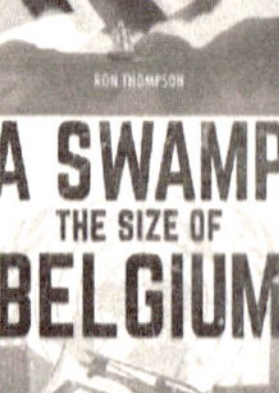

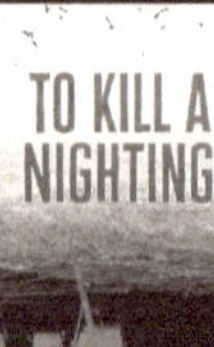

DOUBLE‡DAGGER

— www.doubledagger.ca —

Double Dagger Books is Canada's only military-focused publisher. Conflict and warfare have shaped human history since before we began to record it. The earliest stories that we know of, passed on as oral tradition, speak of war, and more importantly, the essential elements of the human condition that are revealed under its pressure.

We are dedicated to publishing material that, while rooted in conflict, transcend the idea of "war" as merely a genre. Fiction, non-fiction, and stuff that defies categorization, we want to read it all.

Because if you want peace, study war.

www.ingramcontent.com/pod-product-compliance
Lightning Source LLC
Chambersburg PA
CBHW031531310726
48971CB00008B/2440